VENGEANCE
ON THE
MOUNTAIN

Acknowledgements

I couldn't begin to thank everyone who has contributed to my writing over the years but I would be remiss not to acknowledge the invaluable help on this novel from L. Townsend (author of "Searching for Sasquatch Heiress"). If you're a fan of Sasquatch, you'll love his book! You can find his tale of Sasquatch on Amazon by entering the title and his last name or by just searching: ISBN-13: 978-1490312859

In so many ways he has been my mentor and my inspirer. Thanks Lee!

And, thank you to members of the Owyhee County Historical Society, along with its officers and staff. They are always excited to talk of, and show bits and pieces of the area's history. If you are visiting or live in Southwestern Idaho, you owe it to yourself to visit the museum in Murphy, Idaho.

You can learn more about the museum at: http://owyheemuseum.org/

"God promises to make something good out of the storms that bring devastation to your life."

Romans 8:28   The Holy Bible

VENGEANCE
ON THE
MOUNTAIN

NEIL JAMES

If they hadn't seen what happened next, they would never have viewed the rest, and all those people could have lived...

But they did see it!

The two Indian brothers, Lone Squirrel and Running Beaver, far from home and a two-hour ride from the rest of their hunting party had spent two days searching for one of the few remaining buffalo west of the Rocky Mountains. They had seen the tracks three days before and left the hunting party to track it down. They had failed miserably. They found the buffalo, but it had been killed by wolves or cougars or just died of disease. Its bones had been picked clean and the hide destroyed. Disappointed, they had ventured high into the Owyhee Mountains of Southwestern Idaho Territory in search of deer or elk. Again, they had failed and, without food, hunger was driving them back toward the hunting party empty-handed and ashamed. Lone Squirrel had bragged about how they would return with the rare bison and had been laughed at by the leader of the group. He was sarcastic as he told them the tracks were much too old. Now, riding through a draw to avoid detection, they were hidden both from below and above. They were Warm Springs tribesmen and too far south and east. These were the hunting grounds of the Mountain Shoshonis. Warm Springs had no business here and to be found could mean death.

It was the piercing "SCREEEEE" that diverted their attention. At the sound, when first they looked up it was the duck they saw, but not the source of the screech itself. The fast flying mallard heard it too and was trying its best to escape.

The falcon that had been drifting five hundred feet over the sagebrush didn't care. The bird had first caught sight of the greenhead when it was still a quarter of a mile away. Since the fowl was headed on a path that would bring it directly below the falcon, the hunter simply continued to ride the thermal. The bubble of air kept it effortlessly aloft, for it was not in the bird's nature to waste energy.

When the mallard was two hundred yards distant and closing fast, the hunter screeched, made a tight swerve to the left, pulled in its wings and plunged at just over 200 miles per hour. At the last instant its feathers flared to slow its descent and in an explosion of feathers, its hooked beak struck the back of the duck's head, snapping its neck. The falcon leveled off and watched its prey flop to the earth. Gliding, barely topping the sage, it continued to look side to side before landing on an outcropping of rock where the mallard had fallen. With its prey secure in its claws the hunter seemed almost disinterested as it surveyed its surroundings.

The two Warm Springs Indians watched from their horses as the scene played out. The older Lone Squirrel gave a slight smile and nodded to the other. They were hungry. They couldn't see over the small ridge to know where the duck had landed but they heeled their horses up the embankment in hopes of stealing the duck from the falcon.

They topped the embankment just in time to watch the falcon, prey in claws, lift off and ride the air down toward the valley below. They watched until the bird was just a speck, but the older brother's eyes picked up on something much more interesting. A line of white canvas-covered wagons moving slowly along the Snake River. Hunger was forgotten.

PART ONE
1843

From where they sat their horses, the little line of wagons looked an easy target as it wound its way across the sagebrush-covered wastelands. Not too many men and more than enough livestock. The wagon train was following the Snake River plain as it worried its way southwestward from Wyoming. The wide Snake River was a lifeline for travelers and Indians alike as it created a giant smile through the southern part of what would someday become the state of Idaho.

The two Warm Springs Indian brothers were young and anxious to make a name for themselves. True, they had no success as hunters this trip, but that was all about to change. They stayed out of sight as they worked their way down the mountainside. Excited, yet forcing themselves to be patient, they followed and watched and made note of every detail. Once, when his horse gave forth a loud whinny, the younger Running Beaver had leaned forward to clamp his hands around the errant nostrils and mouth. He needn't have bothered; the rattling, clanking, squeaking of the wagons in motion covered all other sounds.

They talked about riding in and cutting out a couple of the horses and riding out again before the tired looking white men could react. That would certainly add to their glory. They reluctantly disposed of that thought in exchange for the bigger treasure. That of bringing the entire hunting party to bear and taking all the livestock. They would certainly be heroes in the eyes of the entire tribe. Yes, like the majestic bird that they had

VENGEANCE ON THE MOUNTAIN

just watched, they too would be patient. They too would wait for the prize.

The wagon train was small. Ten wagons trailing a mixture of milk cows, steers, spare oxen, fifteen mules and six horses. It was a strange looking herd.

Bert Morgan, his broad shoulders slumped in relaxation, sat his horse out in front of the lead wagon. He had no expectation, nor should he have, of the disaster that was about to befall them. He had brought them from Missouri, through the unorganized country that would become Kansas, Nebraska and Wyoming before entering Idaho Territory in Oregon Country. They skirted the northern border of Mexican Territory. Land that would be annexed into the United States just five years later. In 1848 it would become the future states of Nevada, Utah and California.

Making stops at Fort Laramie, Fort Hall and headed to Fort Boise to restock on supplies, the train was following the Snake River, the going slow, hot and difficult.

Bert Morgan was not only the wagon master or more commonly called 'Cap'n' as was custom, but on a mission for himself as well.

Four head of oxen on each wagon clomped along pulling their loads. Men walked alongside their respective lead ox and, with a long stick, poking and tapping, kept the animals moving in the right direction. The wagons were of the schooner type and most had no seats up front. Occupants either walked or rode uncomfortably inside. Across the flat plains, most had at least one rocking chair set up at the back of the wagon bed. Thus, the women could take a break and, in a constant shaking, rocking, bumping motion, rest occasionally. Evenings found the chair placed next to a cooking fire.

Most of the furniture, wood stoves and other heavy items had been left along the trail as the party started into and across the southern Rocky Mountain range. All had held on to their cooking equipment and some few necessities for their future homes. The wagons were so small inside as to only accommodate the possessions. There was little if any room for sleeping. At night, each family erected a canvas tent while older boys usually slept on bedrolls under their wagon or, weather permitting, under the stars.

Two young outriders, sons of the Jason Henry wagon, followed the expedition behind the livestock, urging them along. On occasion, one of the animals would decide to wander away from the group and the tired boys would argue over who should retrieve it. Two of the wagons, with the canvas pulled tight in back to discourage the fog of dust, had lead-ropes that led saddle horses. The pace was slow going. Six of the women and all the children that were old enough to keep up, trudged along beside the wagons. Each step kicked up a small eruption of powdery dust. Often the dust was so intrusive bandanas were worn over the nose and mouth.

Only rarely did any of the riders and walkers look at their surroundings. At an average of two to three miles per hour, the landscape changed slowly. For those afoot, keeping track of where they placed their next step was paramount. A broken ankle or punctured foot would cause not only pain but could be deadly.

In the back of her wagon Martha Jean Brackett held a small boy in her arms. He was nearly a year old. He looked up at her with big adoring eyes as she sang to him. Martha Jean was riding in the wagon beside her husband. He reached over and patted her small hand. She rolled her hand into his and gave it a squeeze. Bernard Brackett, the only man not walking with the oxen, was mending from a near month old injury.

Bernie had been greasing a wheel when the block slipped, and its full weight had crashed down on his foot. It rolled off but the damage was done. It would be at least another week before he could begin to walk with the aid of a cane. A spunky boy from the Gavinetti wagon was doing his best to guide their oxen while Bernie was laid up.

Bernie leaned back and closed his eyes. He was thinking back to when he first brought up the subject to his family. They were sitting on blankets under the big shade tree on an unusually warm April day. The conversation had been light-hearted and continuous. Martha Jean, then just engaged to Bernie, had been invited to join the family picnic after church. At a lull in the talk Bernie took a deep breath and launched into his announcement.

"Well", he said, "Martha Jean and me, we've been talking some about going west."

His mother stopped chewing a bite of pie, swallowed hard and looked at him in disbelief. His father laid down the knife with which he was about to take a second piece. Martha Jean kept a steady fix on her fiancé. No one said a word. Bernie's grandfather swallowed what he was chewing and cleared his throat.

"Well, now, that would be an adventure for sure. When do you consider you might take on this trip?"

"Well, we're fixin' to be married the fourth of June so we thought maybe next spring. We thought we might pack up and catch a wagon train out of Independence in Missouri. We been readin' up on that Oregon country. Free land for the takin' and lots of small towns springin' up. By then, Martha Jean will be done with her nurse schoolin' and me, bein' a barber, well, we been figurin' we could go to one of them towns and be right successful takin' care of the folks. Have us a piece of land to farm, too."

By then, his mother had found her voice and began to list off all the reasons she could come up with about why they shouldn't make a trip like that. There was danger and the probability that they might never see their families again. Of course, both fell on somewhat deaf ears.

Bernie looked to his grandfather, "Gramps, what's your thinkin' on it?"

William Brackett, at seventy-two years old, still with a full head of coal black hair, was capable of a full day's work and was known for his solid wisdom. It was he, who, after losing his wife to a fever over two decades earlier, had decided to make the move to the Midwest. His son and new bride hurriedly decided to go with him.

"Well," said the senior Mr. Brackett, "Don't much hold regrets for the chances I took. Nope, my regrets are mainly for the ones I didn't take. If I took a chance and things didn't work out, well, I tried to learn from it and not make the same mistake again. It's the chances I didn't take that I regret. A man always wonders what good might have come from those missed prospects."

Bernie looked to his father who nodded agreement. His mother sighed and took another bite of pie. It was decided.

Bernard and Martha Jean left their families in Iowa and made their way to Independence, Missouri. That was four months ago. The trip west was a dream come true that had been two years in the making. All was working just as they planned. They had read and re-read all the brochures and had chosen the Missouri To Oregon Transport Company as their guide outfit. They knew it would be rough. They had planned on making the trip the year before but Martha Jean was with child so they decided to wait.

The following year, they spent two weeks in Independence, waiting for the Missouri To Oregon Transport Company's next wagon train to depart. While there they sold their old farm wagon and work horses and purchased a prairie schooner along with six head of oxen. They had considered buying a larger Conestoga wagon but were advised that the lighter schooner was better for the trip to Oregon. They were told that most of the trip would require just four head of oxen to pull their wagon but should have another in case of loss. The extras would be herded along by outriders with other wagon train stock. They were also warned that taking a baby on this long and difficult trip was not suggested. Bernard and Martha Jean were young and confident and anxious to get their life started in the west. They were not deterred.

Even now, on this dry Snake River campo, despite Bernie's injury, enthusiasm had not diminished. The wagons had made their way across the endless plains and through Indian country without much problem except for the unrelenting boredom. The convoy had crossed the dreaded Rocky Mountains and only lost one wagon and one ox. Two children had died of dysentery and it was feared that one youngster might be suffering from cholera. But Martha Jean Brackett had been keeping track of the child and her training as a nurse told her it was not the dreaded disease. There was great relief with her diagnosis.

Finally, it seemed, the troop of settlers was almost there. Almost to Oregon and their new homes. To them, mostly farmers, the promise of rich farm ground for the taking was better than the promise of the gold sought by prospectors, or the seemingly endless supply of furs, being taken by trappers.

To the Warm Springs Indian, Lone Squirrel, who had been watching them for the last seven hours, his notion of gold was in the form of the livestock that went with the white man. He had sent his younger brother to tell Man of the Horse, the band's leader, of what they had stumbled across. His horse nickered once again but now Lone Squirrel, sitting in the shade of a juniper tree, paid no attention. He realized the wagons were too far below and making too much noise for the people to hear much of anything. Every hour or so, he would climb back on his horse and move forward to a secluded position and wait for the wagons to reappear. Soon, he was certain, Man of the Horse, as anxious for recognition as himself, would join him with the entire war party. Today, his people would have their gold and he and his brother would get much of the credit.

The day had been long, the afternoon hot, everybody tired and looking forward to the evening's rest. As the sun slipped farther and farther in the northwestern sky they began to pull into a grove of trees.

Bert Morgan had made this very trip before. Each of the past two years, he had contracted with the Missouri To Oregon Transport Company – the MTO as people called it - to lead wagon trains to the Oregon Territory. Even these weren't his first ventures from the Midwest. He had trapped along the Snake River and its tributaries for several seasons before taking out the first wagon train. He knew the route. He knew where he wanted to camp each of the nights. Marked out plainly on a crude but accurate map that he kept in his leather 'possibles' case. Every man in the train knew where that map was kept. Bert Morgan was a realist. He knew that if anything happened to him, somebody would need the map to proceed. Every man on the train, having studied the map, knew, at least generally, where they were headed. They knew the major landmarks. They knew where water should be found. They knew the most likely spots for an Indian raid. Morgan had been successful because of his leadership and knowledge. Knowledge hard earned, for Bert Morgan had been many things in his life. While still a teenager, he had signed on to fight in the Ute and Apache wars. After three years of heavy, often hand to hand fighting, he was a seasoned combatant. He had been a sheriff, a dragoon officer, and a Texas Ranger. From his military days, he had learned an important lesson. If you want your troops to work in unison and at their best, make sure they know why they are fighting, who they are fighting and how the battle will most likely progress. Using this philosophy, Morgan allied most all of the men in his wagon trains by educating them about what they would probably encounter.

So it was that the train of 1843 was surprised but not unprepared when the attack came.

It happened along the banks of the Snake River without warning. It came from a band of young Warm Springs comprised of approximately 40 warriors. It was a surprise because Bert Morgan had not anticipated hostile actions from the Snake River tribes. Still, as soon as the first arrow found its target and the ten-year-old boy fell face down in the dust, the alarm was shouted out and everyone on the train followed a drill that they had practiced several times. The wagons were pulled into a semi-circle within the trees. The river was at their back offering some degree of buffer. The trees were not large but made it difficult for the raiders to have clear shots. Following constant orders from Bert Morgan, the pioneers fought effectively. The bodies of the young, inexperienced warriors began to build in number. Too many of them felt they were invincible and made frivolous runs at the protectors, hoping to collect coup but ultimately ending in their demise. The battle continued on and off for hours. The Warm Springs would retreat, regroup and attack again. Each attack came in a different way. Some straight on. Some from one side or another. Some with small groups rushing from all sides at once. More than a few times, shots were heard from the two men stationed to watch the river. A young warrior or two would try to sneak along the riverbank to gain a rear advantage and be shot by the guardians of the waterway. By the time dark was nearing, only one of the wagon train's men and the boy had been killed but three had been wounded, one badly enough that he could no longer fight. Still, they were holding their own.

There is a widespread myth that Indians never attacked at night. Nobody told the Warm Springs. The young warriors stopped their attacks about an hour before full dark. They gathered just out of rifle range and watched and waited. About two hours after, with a cloud filled sky, no stars or moon to help the waggoneers see their approach, the final attack took place. Bert Morgan had ordered that the men sleep in shifts with half always in position and alert. The plan was a good one, but the pure darkness could not be overcome. The Warm Springs warriors had no problem getting within ten feet of the wagons. Well versed in the art of stealth, they simply waited for the signal. When Man of the Horse gave a war whoop, ten arrows found their marks and eight of the wagon train's 17 men fell dead. The screams instantly brought the other men out of their slumber. They strained their eyes but found no targets. One by one they were cut down from the darkness, without retaliation. Because he was closest to the perimeter, Bert Morgan was one of the first to be hit. With two arrows in his body, he still struggled to get up. He reached for his revolver and got off one shot before a young warrior smashed a club into his head from behind. For Bert Morgan, the battle was over.

Suddenly, upwards of thirty warriors were running through the interior of the encampment, slashing and clubbing. When the last defensive shot had been discharged and all the defenders lay dead or dying, the raiders lit their way with torches to rummage through the belongings, pilfering clothes, blankets, leather, tools, jewelry, food, even the canvas that covered the wagons and anything else they perceived of value. They also took money when found, because already, there were white men, mostly French trappers, who would trade goods of value to the Indians for the white man's money.

They brought in the mules and horses and loaded them with their booty. The torches were tossed to the wagons and amongst whoops and hollers, and pounding of hooves, the Warm Springs and their booty disappeared into the night. Man of the Horse knew that their luck would give out if they were found by a band of Snake Indians that lived along the river. He ordered his dead and wounded picked up and to quickly head back to the northwest. The dust and smoke from the raid slowly settled. Then, only the of crackling flames sounded against the lapping water of the slow flowing Snake River.

By the time a dim eastern gray began to overcome the total darkness, only two of the pioneers were still unscathed. Martha Jean Brackett and her year-old son, Clayton. She had no way of knowing that all the Indians had left. She was terrified that some might be searching the area. She and the baby were hidden on the river bank in some reeds but, as quiet overtook the darkness and the fighting stopped, she had slipped into the water, waist deep, and slowly worked her way downstream. But was it far enough? When it began to get light, the heartbroken young widow realized that she would need to move. With dawn, Martha Jean and her baby could be exposed. Once more, she slipped into the water and began drifting with the current but always keeping her baby out of the chilly water. Finally, far down the river, shaking from the cold she thought she must get onto the bank to warm up or she would surely perish.

Looking all around, and with great effort, she pulled herself onto the bank. Exhausted, she lay back. The sun reached over the distant mountains and crept slowly across the sagebrush desert across the river, finally finding its way to Martha Jean's shivering body. Slowly, ever so slowly, she began to feel its effect.

Southward behind her and reaching a distance of forty feet to accomplish, the bank gently rose some ten feet above. She couldn't see over and beyond the embankment. The baby seemed content and was having a hard time keeping his eyes open. He had tried to stand but fell with a yet-to-be-developed sense of balance. She listened intently. Not a sound beyond the slight lapping of the river and what sounded like tree leaves gently shimmering in the light breeze someplace beyond her sight. The baby's voice was becoming a bit less happy. Martha Jean realized it had been a very long time since she had fed the little fellow. Twenty minutes later, when the baby began to lose interest in eating, his belly full, she rocked him until he fell asleep. Assured that he would not move for a while, Martha Jean worked her way to the top of the bank on her hands and knees. Cautiously, looking over the top, she looked for some sign that would warn of danger. She didn't know how many might have survived the raid. She knew her Bernie did not. He had died in her arms after telling her to escape to the river and hide.

A small copse of cottonwoods stood on the banks of a small creek that fed into the Snake. She neither heard nor saw a thing except miles of sagebrush slowly giving way to high mountains. She knew they had been headed for Fort Boise but had no idea how far that might be. She couldn't even remember if Bernie had told her if it was on the Snake or some other river.

Her mind told her to wait, make sure the Indians were gone. This collided with an equally strong need to get back to the wagons to see if she could help the folks that were still alive. It had been after midnight that she heard the last gun shots. Perhaps an hour or more after she made her way to the river. The triumphant shouts and seeming celebration of the Indians had subsided not long after. She didn't know what happened thereafter but, for a long time she could see the light of the burning wagons. She moved back to her baby and lay back to soak in the sun while she tried to decide what to do. With the warmth of the morning came a crushing fatigue. She was tired. So very, very tired. She turned onto her back and pulled the child onto her chest. The baby babbled groggily and tried to tell her something but didn't yet have words that could be understood. He was soon back to sleep. Martha Jean knew she needed to come to a decision on what action to take but she was so exhausted. She thought that for just a moment she could close her eyes. Just for a moment. She watched white clouds move through the blue sky as her consciousness drifted away with them.

Martha Jean jerked awake. Escaping those awful dreams of her husband bleeding and coughing up blood. Tears streaming down her cheeks.

The baby! Where was Clay? Martha Jean still lay on her back but the baby was not on her chest. She snapped into a sitting position and desperately looked to each side and then to the river. Instantly she was in a panic as it hit her that the baby may have crawled into the flow of current. She stood up and started down to the water. Suddenly she was jerked backwards and onto the ground. Confusion took hold as she tried to grasp what had happened.

The voice was harsh. The words foreign to her ears. She looked up from where she was lying. The sun showed only a silhouette of what was obviously a very big man. She started to jump up but a foot shoved her back to the ground. This time she was rolled to the side. When she looked up the sun was no longer creating the silhouette and she could clearly see the man. Instantaneously, two emotions grabbed her. First, panic! Secondly, anger! The monster held her baby! This time she jumped up so quickly that it caught the big Indian off guard. Before he could react, Martha Jean had her hands on the baby he was holding and trying to pull it from his grasp. His hold was tight. With his free hand he backhanded her across her mouth, and she tumbled to the ground once again. Immediately she jumped up again. This time he put out his hand to stop her. She stopped short, screaming at him in. He reached to his belt and pulled out his skinning knife, holding it toward her. She screamed again and took one step toward him and then froze. Now the tears and pleading sounds came pouring out of her. She dropped to her knees and held out her hands, imploring for him to give her the baby.

He turned his back to her and started up the bank. She kept pleading but followed him. Topping the incline, he walked over to a horse that had been tethered to a sagebrush. She immediately knew the horse. She had watched Bert Morgan ride that horse every day for months. Still holding the baby, the big savage ignored the stirrups and seemingly without effort, swung onto the saddle. Without looking at her he started riding away at a slow walk. She screamed at him again and started running after him. The baby was crying, she was screaming, and the big black horse was a bit skittish without its regular rider. Purposefully keeping the horse at a slow pace, he showed no surprise when she caught up to them and grabbed hold of the tie down strings at the back of the saddle. Once, she tried to grab hold of the baby and he knocked her hands away without looking at her. From then on, she just hung on to the piece of rawhide string and stumbled along beside. She had quit screaming but couldn't help a grunt now and then when she stumbled. Once, she tripped over a clump of bunch grass and fell with a thud to the ground. He didn't stop or look back at her. She yelled at him to wait but he didn't acknowledge her. A bit later she was back, huffing and puffing, holding onto the string.

For over an hour, the big Indian rode on, unwavering in his pace. Finally, they came to a spring. A small pool of water had formed below the trickle that came from deep in the ground. He brought the black to a stop and swinging his right leg over the neck of the horse, slid to the ground. Exhausted and barely able to stand, her eyes begged for her baby. He motioned for her to join the horse in drinking from the pool. She reluctantly dropped to her hands and knees and drank. It took all of her strength to regain her stance. She wiped sweat from her eyes. Still holding the now silent baby, the Indian stood by a granite rock about twenty feet away. Shaped like a loaf of bread, it was at least three times the size of the horse and provided shade on the side toward the spring. Martha Jean started to the baby but the Indian motioned her to sit in the shade at the base of the rock. She did as she was told with her back against its coolness. Holding her arms out for the baby, tears streaming down her cheeks, Martha Jean was surprised when he handed down the little guy. She looked at him with grateful eyes and hugged pint-sized Clayton Brackett tightly. She kept her eyes on her captor as he walked to the spring and stepped to the other side of the little pool. He watched her as he drank. Then he sat down with his back leaning against the trunk of a juniper tree. She watched him watching her and finally began to look at their surroundings. They were headed into the foothills of the mountains. She wondered if he would kill them if she couldn't keep up. She wondered if he would kill them anyway, wondered why he was keeping them alive even now.

She tried to take in the features of her captor. He was tall, taller than her husband who had been considered a big man. This man might be six feet three or four inches. His shoulders were broad, and his chest stretched the buckskin shirt. He was definitely Indian but not as dark as the ones who had raided her wagon train. He had a leather necklace with some sort of ornament. An animal tooth she guessed. His hair was long and unbraided and so black that it shone in the sunlight. Unlike the other warriors that had attacked the wagon train, he wore no paint. His feet were bound in laced up moccasins. His breeches were of stained rawhide or buckskin that reached just below his knees. His eyes were dark under thick, black brows and yet not unfriendly. His high cheekbones led down to full lips and a prominent chin. Under different circumstances she might have thought him to be handsome.

He sat there for maybe ten minutes before getting up. Instinctively she stood up as well, pulling the baby closer, dreading his taking the youngster away once more. He motioned for her to bring the baby to the horse where he was standing. She hesitated and again, with more assertiveness, he motioned for her approach. She slowly walked over to him, all the while, without knowing it, shaking her head, silently begging him not to take the baby from her. He held out his hands and with tears streaming, she handed over her little charge. He motioned for her to get on the horse. When she showed confusion he simply reached out with his free arm, grabbed her around her waist and swung her up into the saddle. Before she could grasp what was happening, he raised the baby to her, took the reins and led the horse out toward the high peaks beyond.

For hours he continued to walk, never did he speed up or slow down. She did notice that his pace was considerably faster than when she had been the one walking. Her legs hurt from the earlier trek. Her left foot was covered in dried blood from the wound suffered when she had fallen. Her dress had a long tear in it over her knee. The scrape on her leg had bled for a while. She was beginning to feel the need to nurse the baby but was worried about exposing herself. The baby began to cry. The Indian never looked back. Finally, she decided that she had no other choice and began the feeding. Not once did he look back. She relaxed. Riding up here on the big black horse gave her time to think. She decided that if he was going to do her harm, he would have done it by now. She also decided that escape was not an option until he left her unguarded with the horse and baby. That was not probable.

The sun moved across the sky as she took in the heat waves shimmering above the sand. Off to their right an eagle made its call, momentarily catching her attention as it circled in a thermal. She did her best to protect the baby from the sun and the ever-present swarm of tiny desert flies that followed like a pack of wolves. Constantly, they tried to get to moisture of the baby's eyes. She had taken off his little coat and tried to hold it above the boy's head to provide shade. He squirmed constantly and whimpered, yelled and fell silent. At last he settled down with the motion of the horse and slept.

In the distance, just where it appeared that the landscape began to change and they would climb into the mountains proper, she could make out what looked to be a stand of willows. She was thirsty and the sight of the greenery seemed only to intensify the dryness of her tongue. She focused on what she hoped would be water and after an eternity she could clearly see the oasis drawing near. It turned out to be a fairly good-sized stream coming out of a canyon that had been hidden from her earlier. The Indian led them into a stand of cottonwood trees where the shade cooled her face and hands. He stopped in a clearing that had obviously been a campsite for many previous generations. Grass grew green alongside the creek and when he had pulled her from the horse and let it drink, he took the bridle off, loosened the cinch and, with the lariat that Bert Morgan had always carried on the saddle, tethered the black to a tree. The big brute immediately went to grazing.

With the baby beside her on the cool sand of the stream's edge, stretching out on her stomach, she drank long and deep. When she could hold no more, she sat up and removed her shoes. The water was so cold that her feet quickly began to ache. She dipped her hand in the stream and gingerly patted its coolness on the baby's face and neck as he giggled in delight. Martha Jean looked around to see where the Indian had gone but couldn't see him. She wondered if she should gather up the infant and try to escape. But to where? She had no idea where she was or where she would go. Before she could even finish her thoughts, he was back. No sound. He was gone and then he was there. She didn't see from where he came. She had looked to her left and when looking back, he stood gazing down at her. She stripped the baby, washed his diaper and after letting it warm some, wiped his little bottom with the cloth. She rewashed it and hung it over some branches to dry. For now, he would be free to crawl around naked.

He wondered at the woman's blonde hair. Never had he seen such as this. She had it curled up in a blob atop her head for some reason. All the women he knew took great pride in displaying their long black hair. Evidently, where she came from, the yellow hair was an embarrassment, so she tried to keep it hidden beneath the piece of colored cloth that now dangled on her back. Her dress looked ridiculous to him. What good was it? Much too wide and blossomed to allow for good work. The women he knew wore practical clothes that aided in their daily chores. But he had to admit that except for her white man skin, when she washed off the mud and sweat and dust at the spring, she was not as ugly as he had been told most white women were. The fact was that this was the first one he had ever seen up close. There was something about her that stirred strange feelings within him. Not lust, but a feeling that he needed to watch over her. Her baby was strange looking, too. Not bad really, but different. He wasn't quite sure what he would do with the two of them. Maybe trade them for a white man's gun.

Since his wife died of disease a year ago, Buha, as he was called, had grieved. He had wanted a son. He had wanted his wife in his tepee until they were both old. Now, neither of those two wishes would be granted by the gods. His father, the man of wisdom in his tribe, had said another would fill his heart. He said another would bring him a son.

Buha had high respect for all that his father said, but, no other woman in his village had piqued any interest in him. His band that had become known as the Mountain Shoshonis were seasonal nomads that moved two times a year, following game and edible plant seasons. The Northern Shoshoni that stayed at the lower elevations had women that he could take but he had no interest in them, either.

His clan had mostly peaceful relations, although sometimes strained, with the other tribes and clans in the area. They had no use for the Warm Springs tribes that stayed mainly to the northwest of them, although on occasion, those Warm Springs would follow the great river south, as had the raiding party that had burned the wagons.

When *his* people raided, it was for a reason. If his band had raided the wagon train, moving silently at night, they would have done only what was necessary to take the livestock and move quickly away. He found it disgusting when he came across the burned-out wagon train from which he assumed the woman and baby had come. Obviously, the men, women and children had been slaughtered just for bragging rights. He had run across a small band of Warm Springs that he believed had taken part in the raid. Out of their sight, he watched as they passed. He could see that they carried at least a dozen dead and could see several more that were obviously wounded. What wisdom was there in that?

Also, he mused, they had missed this great beast of a horse. The finest he had ever ridden and probably the best he had ever seen. He couldn't help an inner smile at that thought.

The fact was that Buha, like his father, Great Bear had little or no feeling of brotherhood for any other band or tribe. Their allegiance belonged only to their own people, the Mountain People.

He was a warrior and probably the best of the many tribes within three hundred miles in any direction, although he never considered that. Self-pride was not in his thought process. In his twenty-five summers, he had fought in many battles. Some were with other tribes. Some with white men trying to run his band out of their seasonal holdings along the great river, or an occasional raid to get livestock, although those had been few. Seldom were raids needed. The mountains provided game in plentiful numbers from the time the snow melted in the spring until the first flurries in the fall that told his people it was time to move to the river below for the winter. They followed what Great Bear had learned from the Crows and the Nez Perce and bred their own horses.

In all these battles, he had been wounded just one time. The arrow, shot by a Warm Springs raiding party, had only grazed his left arm just above the elbow. He didn't even realize it happened until one of his warriors pointed it out after the battle had concluded.

Buha, like his father, when in battle as a warrior, was ruthless. But, while he understood why some tribes used torture as a means of frightening their enemies, it was not part of the mountain people's nature to do so. However, when he fought, he fought to kill. His father had taught him to use whatever means most effective to kill his enemy. When he killed, he killed without a second thought and without remorse. This he had learned well from Great Bear and this he would teach his sons if ever he had sons.

He was tough through and through and yet, like many of his clan, he was soft hearted in so many ways. He was especially patient with the children of the tribe. He would let them wrestle with him and pretend that they were winning. He did this much in the same way that his father and uncle had done with him. Through this wrestling, the boys learned how to fight. He also spent time teaching the fatherless older boys how to hunt and fish while their mothers and sisters were gathering camas root or working the deer and elk hides.

He was now well recognized as the future chief. Throughout the tepees of the village, all knew of and respected the father's wisdom. He had passed much of that wisdom to his son and now, as Great Bear neared the end of his days, the people felt at peace with their future leader. His clan numbered about 180 men, women and children. Of those, sixty were warriors. Four more would be added within the next moon as the young men passed their requirements to be considered full-fledged warriors.

His was a very large band. Most clans could not support anywhere close to that number. It had been his father's wisdom in breaking with tradition and choosing the high mountains as their spring, summer and autumn camp that allowed for such a big settlement. The hunting in the high country was abundant as were the balsam roots and mountain berries. For his entire life the clan had known the goodness offered there. There was no need for the young men to leave to find their own way as was the case with his lowland brothers where not enough food could be secured. Supporting more than twenty or thirty family members down below was a challenge.

The clan didn't start out as Shoshoni. In fact, Buha was pure Comanche. His father, Great Bear had brought them from the plains of New Mexico many seasons before. In his Comanche village, Great Bear had been forced to fight with his own cousin for the hand of Buha's mother. The contest ended quickly as the cousin was long on confidence and short on the fighting skills he thought he possessed. Holding the knife at his cousin's throat and at the urging of all the other braves to finish the disliked challenger, Great Bear had instead stood and walked away. His cousin had run to pick up his knife and threw it at the back of Great Bear. A warning shout came just in time to allow him to dodge sideways as the blade swished by. This time he didn't hesitate. His throw was on target and for just a moment, before tumbling to the ground, the challenger looked down in stunned disbelief at the knife that had plunged deep into his heart.

It was after this event that Great Bear decided to take his small clan far away from the land of the Comanche. It consisted of only his wife, brother, his two sisters and their husbands, his four best friends and their several wives and children.

Although known as the Mountain Shoshonis, Great Bear and his tribe were actually now a mix of Comanche, Bannock and Shoshoni. Great Bear had brought his tribe to the Owyhee Mountains before Buha was born. He had heard that the Comanche's cousins across the big mountains would welcome them. When they arrived, they found little in common and no love of the Fisheaters, Diggers and other Snake Indians making up most of the Shoshonis and Bannocks. He didn't want the constant moving in search of the bare minimum of substance. After a short time, he took his band to find better hunting in the high country.

He was initially scorned by the rest of the tribes as being foolish to leave the river. However, as times continued to be hard in the lowlands over the following years, more began to find the mountain clan and ask for admission. Great Bear and his council were careful who they allowed to join their band. Most were sent away, but the clan still continued to grow and multiply. Those rejected became bitter but had not the heart to take on Great Bear.

Only when the snows came did the Mountain People make the four-thousand-foot descent to the mouth of the Owyhee River at its confluence with the Snake. Here they fished and ate the reserve of summer's bounty that had been dried, crushed into flour and preserved for this time. The winters felt long and most waited impatiently to return to the mountains. Time was filled as the old men told their stories and passed along the history of the tribes. With three different tribe's stories to be related, the young found a lot to learn. It was then, also, that they traded with the other bands, worked on tools and weapons, mended clothes. Still they hunted. Deer followed the same annual migration to the lower country and were taken when the gods were with the hunters.

It was the fierceness with which Buha's father had fought that led his clan to call him the Great Bear. Now, that same reputation for fierceness had been earned by his son. Now, he too had earned a name for his unbeatable skill in combat. It was said that Great Bear's son must have special power not given to ordinary men. The tribe believed he got his power from the great medicine of the gods. His name had been Little Bear after his father, but now the people changed his name to Buha, or loosely translated, *he who possesses Spirit Medicine*.

Because of Buha's great leadership in battle and his well thought out input in tribal matters, it was accepted that he also inherited his father's wisdom. Everyone would grieve when Great Bear died but they were confident that they would be well protected under Buha.

Great Bear, they knew, had been lying near death for several days. He had said he would wait for the return of his son, Buha, who had been gone for nearly a week and did not know of his father's illness. Only then, said Great Bear, could he pass on to the sky spirits.

The Indian went to the horse and tightened the cinch. He put the bridle back in place and untied the lariat. He walked to the creek and leaning down, cupped water in his hand and drank. When he stood up, he motioned for Martha Jean to do the same. She arose and carried the baby to the creek and drank. He put her and the baby back on the horse and led the way out of the trees and back into the heat of the high desert foothills.

The sun was dropping low when he next drew to a stop. A small gurgle of water streamed down the rock face of granite that loomed a hundred feet above. From the horse he removed the saddle and bridle. This time he took the lead-rope from the saddle and secured it around the horse's two front feet to act as hobbles. The big black didn't object. Martha Jean knew he had often been left to graze in such a manner. He munched bunch grass that grew next to the tiny brook.

Martha Jean drank from the trickle of water and sat down beside it with her back against the wall of rock. She was in the shade now and as before, the coolness of the stone felt good. Already the day's heat was retreating and after once again washing out little Clayton's diaper, she put his jacket back on him.

It was past time to feed him and she didn't know what to do. The Indian had gathered some firewood a bit away from the little stream and now was looking directly at her. She got up her nerve and told him she had to feed the baby. His expression did not change, and it was clear he had no idea what she was trying to tell him. Nor, she decided, did he care.

Then he pointed at her and made a downward motion with both hands. *Stay where you are.* She nodded at him and he turned and disappeared behind a stand of willows. She took the opportunity to feed the baby and relieve herself behind a tree. He was gone at least an hour. When he came back, he found her and the baby just where he had left them. Along with some kind of roots, he carried two cottontail rabbits that dangled by their hind legs from his left hand. He motioned for her to join him where he was striking a shiny black rock against another stone. The sparks flew into a little pile of dried grass and smoke began to appear. He blew gently on the smoke and it burst into flame. He layered this with small sticks and then larger ones.

By then she was holding the baby by the fire. The Indian pulled out his skinning knife and flipped it, catching it by the blade, so as to present it to her by the handle. She looked at him inquisitively. He pointed to the rabbits on the ground and again held the knife out to her. Understanding, she nodded, straightened to her full five foot two inches and said in a strong voice with a note of contempt, "I'll show you; I know exactly how to do this." With some degree of satisfaction, she hoped he understood the tone if not the words. She sat Clay on the ground beside her. For the first time in the horrendous hours of the past day and night, she felt a bit of confidence. Martha Jean had cooked many such rabbits over campfires during the past few months. She took the knife, picked up the first rabbit and went to work.

The Indian went to the stand of willows and broke off branches to construct a spit over the fire. Martha Jean walked to the stream where she pulled out the entrails, washed out the carcasses and finished the skinning without difficulty. She rinsed off the knife and handed it back to the big red man as she returned to the fire. He used it to sharpen another stick and handed that to her. She ran the green branch through the bodies of the rabbits and placed it between the two forked sticks that he had planted on either side of the fire.

Young Clay began to fuss and before she could react, the Indian had placed him on his lap. Martha Jean started to reach for the youngster, and he shook his head. He pointed to the fire and then to a dead willow where he had gotten the original fire makings. To her mind, wood collecting was a man's job. Finding herself with a slight frown, all at once her entire disposition changed. She was no longer afraid for the lives of herself and son. At least, not for the time being. Suddenly, she was sure he would not harm them as long as she did as he said.

Again, he motioned to the wood source. She nodded and went her way. As the fire burned and the coals built up hot, she turned the stick that held the rabbits. He sat and watched. He had given the baby back to her and now, when the rabbits were cooked, she handed Clayton back to him. He received him without the slightest thought, and she took the rabbits off the fire and rested them on a nearby rock to cool. She held out her hand, indicating his knife. He looked at her for a moment and then removed it from its sheath and handed it to her handle first. She used it to cut the two rabbits into pieces. She could see his confusion concluding that he would have saved the effort and just eaten the things off the stick. She could see that he thought this white woman did things in a strange manner. He didn't appear to find her aggravating but interesting. Even amusing she thought. He appeared to smile to himself as he watched her.

Martha Jean found a slab of shale rock, flat and light, approximating the size of a serving platter. She was proud of herself to have brought a bit of class to this wild place.

She may be held captive by a savage, but she didn't have to eat like one. Both ate their fill and there was still a bit left.

The Indian pulled off a tiny piece and put it in the baby's mouth. Martha Jean immediately reacted. His sharp look said STOP! She had no way of knowing that Indian babies were eating small amounts of meat by the time they were seven or eight months old.

Martha Jean nervously watched as the baby happily used his few teeth to chew bite after bite of the stuff. She was amazed. Her training and all her upbringing said that babies should only have liquids at this age. She would be nervous over the next day or two to see how he handled this new food-type.

When she had gathered enough wood to keep the fire banked through the night, she wrapped the baby in the saddle blanket as the evening turned cool. Nestled beside him, she watched a shooting star cross above and thought of Bernie and the many friends she had lost. A tear found its way down her cheek. The big Indian reclined on the other side of the fire and slept easily.

The sun was not yet up when the baby awoke and wanted to be fed. By the time little Clay was finished, the Indian had saddled the horse and removed the hobbles. The air was still cool. Puffy clouds drifted across the rising sun and somewhere in the distance a crow complained of a coyote hunting too near.

He led them out of the camp and into the mountains. The climb was steady but most of the time not steep. Now that the fear was gone, Martha Jean began to grieve over the loss of Bernie. He was a good man. She loved him as her dearest and most cherished friend. She knew she had never been *in love* with him the way some of her friends gushed about their beaus, but he had certainly loved her with all his heart and soul and that was enough. They had in common a dream of going west. They had gotten married and worked for two years to save up the money to make the trip west. She missed him greatly. He had such wonderful dreams and plans and she had shared each one of them. Now, even if she survived, none of those dreams would come true. She wiped away the tears and looked at the baby. She resolved to not look back at what could have been but only concentrate on what she could do to protect Clay Brackett, the only thing she had left of Bernie. Maybe she could escape. Maybe she would someday get back to her own kind. For now, they just needed to take one hour at a time, one minute at a time, and survive.

The sun had peaked and traversed to the west. Another three hours, it would move to the northwest and begin its descent. The climb had become steeper and, in some places, he had her dismount and walk. More than once she slipped and fell. After the first fall the Indian had taken the child and carried Clay himself. When she was too tired to go on, she sat down on a rock to rest. The Indian must have heard the lack of footsteps and stopped without ever turning around. The baby began to fuss but they were at the top of the steepest climb. He motioned for her to again mount the horse. Once in the saddle, he handed her the baby and led on.

They were now on a well-traveled trail that broke over a saddle into a bowl type valley. She was shocked to see numerous tepees and hogans. Fifty, sixty or more. As they drew closer, she could see kids playing by a creek and women working on various tasks. Here and there were men, dressed much like her captor, sitting cross legged in small circles around campfires. When he led them into the midst of all this, several youngsters ran to his side. He walked to a tepee roughly in the center of the others and stopped. He dropped the lead-rope and reins and stooping down, entered the hide covered structure. As Martha Jean sat there, not knowing what to do, several women began to gather around her, all talking at once and pointing to her hair. They were also very interested in her baby. One reached up to touch his head and Martha Jean instinctively pulled him away. The woman pulled back but responded in what sounded like angry words.

The cover to the entrance opened and the big Indian emerged. He had a grim look. He gathered the reins and lead-rope and led the horse to another tepee just a bit farther into the village. When he stopped, he motioned for the woman and baby to dismount and indicated she should go into the tepee. When she hesitated, he abruptly pulled her down and gave her just the slightest of pushes in the direction of the opening. He then turned and walked away with the horse.

It took a minute or so for Martha Jean's eyes to adjust to the darkness, but her nose was immediately assaulted with the smell of smoke combined with animal hides. It was not an odor she found pleasant. The baby was asleep, not even awakened by the rough dismount. She found a deer hide in one corner that felt soft to the touch and laid the baby on it. It was warm inside the dwelling. As her eyes adjusted and she was able to take in the surroundings, nothing appeared complicated. The tepee was round and about fifteen feet across at its base. The floor was just tromped-down, dry grass.

Around the edges were spread animal hides. In the center was a fire pit with wood laid to one side. A much larger pile of wood was stacked against an outside wall. On the sides were hung various items, seemingly used for cooking and hunting. They were all supported by rawhide strings looped through holes in the covering hides. Construction appeared to be several poles that ran from the ground to a central point at the top. These poles were bound together, and a hole was left open at the top to allow smoke to escape. The walls were a combination of branches, leaves and hides. It looked like something that could be constructed in short order and moved easily.

Martha Jean checked the baby and cautiously opened the flap that covered the entrance. There was no sign of the big Indian. The rest of the village had resumed their activities. There was no sign of a guard. It seemed like she could just take the baby and sneak away. The problem was the same here as on the trail. Where would she escape to? At least here, it looked like she would be able to keep the baby warm and fed. As for her, she didn't know what would happen.

It was dark when he reappeared. He walked in and without saying a word, started a fire as he had on the trail. He tossed her a small deerskin bag. Inside was what appeared to be some kind of cured meat. She assumed it was deer or elk. He had already extracted two large pieces for himself and began to rip chunks loose with his teeth and chew on them. He said something. It was without meaning to her. He ripped another bite and indicated she should do the same.

"Alright, so I'm not going to starve. At least not for now."

She realized that she had said this out loud. She looked up at him, but he paid no attention. He had his knife out and was rubbing the blade on a stone as he chewed. She watched. He was very deliberate in his motion. It was almost mesmerizing. The baby was awake and fussing. He was hungry. She picked him up not sure how to handle this. She looked at the Indian. He was looking at her. He showed just a bit of irritation. He pointed to the baby, then to his mouth, cupped his hand under his own breast, pointed to her and gave a definite indication that she should feed the baby.

Slowly she turned around, so she was facing away from her captor, looking at the interior materials of the shelter. She fed the baby and when Clay had finished, she turned around. The Indian was gone and Martha Jean realized she was very tired. She settled down on the deer skin with her son and quickly fell asleep.

She awoke to the sounds of little Clay softly jabbering away to himself. For a moment she didn't remember where she was. She rolled to her side to look. The flickering firelight played across his face. He had two fingers in his mouth and was sucking on them. On the other side of the fire she could make out the Indian, evidently asleep. She had no idea when he had returned. She found it unnerving how he could just come and go without a sound.

The dawn broke onto blue skies and the promise of another warm day. He had left again without comment or acknowledgement that she was even there. Martha Jean had gained some confidence and ventured outside the flap. She sat with her back against the structure talking to the baby. Clay had been crawling for several months and standing up with the aid of something to hold on to. He was leaning against her now. Then, without any warning he just let go and took two steps before falling. He looked at her, giggled and stood up without help. Two more steps, a fall, back up, three steps, a fall, back up, another giggle. He turned around and started back to her. He would have made it had it not been for a small rock that tripped him. He giggled again and resumed his experiment. This time he made it. She was grinning wide when the Indian's shadow fell across them.

With him were two women. One looked to be in her late teens or early twenties, near her own age. The other was considerably older. Maybe fiftyish. She was the one that was talking as they walked closer. She seemed to be in charge. The Indian seemed almost bigger than before as he looked down at the boy standing against Martha Jean and she was sure he almost smiled. Then his face went back to that considered look that he normally carried.

He reached down and picked up the boy. Martha Jean jumped to her feet. He held out a hand commanding that she stay where she stood. Then he handed the boy over to the older woman. She abruptly turned and walked away. Martha Jean immediately yelled out in protest and started to go after them. Her captor stuck out one of his massive arms and stopped her. Then something happened that neither quite understood. He looked at her with a look that told her that it was ok. She instantly knew that it was. She trusted him. She had no idea why but she did. She watched the older woman go back to the tepee where they first stopped the day before. Martha Jean watched as the older woman set the boy on his feet, backed up a few feet, held out her hands. The old woman was smiling and talking to the boy. Clayton, with unsteady steps, waddled to her outstretched fingers.

The young woman with the big Indian now reached out and took her firmly by the arm and gave her a tug to follow. Martha

Jean looked at her and the girl smiled and nodded. With a swish of her long black hair she pointed to the stream. Martha Jean looked up at the Indian and he nodded at her. Together they walked to the stream. Here the young woman stopped and faced Martha Jean. She pointed to her chest and said, "Eloo". Then she pointed to Martha Jean and said something that was obviously a question.

"Martha", said Martha Jean and pointed to her own chest. Then she pointed to the girl and said, "Eloo?" The girl laughed and pointed back and said, "Marta". Then she pointed to herself and said, "Eloo".

They both repeated this once more and both laughed. The girl squatted beside a deer hide lying flat on the grass. It had been stretched and dried. She gave Martha Jean a piece of obsidian that had been sharpened along one side. She showed Martha Jean how to use the shiny black rock to scrape off the hair. The two of them worked all day on the hide. They traded words for various things as they worked. It didn't take long for Marta - Eloo couldn't say the 'th' sound - to realize that this Indian maiden was not only beautiful but very smart and quick to learn. She hoped she could keep up.

Several times during the day, the old woman, the one they called Huzi, the one who kept track of Martha Jean's son, brought the boy to her so she could feed him. Each time, a few of the band's old women would gather around and talk about and point to the boy and his mother and nod, with seeming approval. There was lots of laughing and friendly nudging. These were obviously happy, hardworking people. They were nothing like they had been represented to Martha Jean by the stories she had been reading about the west. She wondered how these seemingly peaceful people could be the same ones that committed such atrocities on her wagon train. How was that possible? Still, she had been with them for only part of two days.

The first time the old lady brought the boy to her he was naked from the waist down like all the other small boys and girls in the village. Obviously, diapers were a waste of time and energy. When a child would poop,

Neil James

the mother, or any other woman that happened to be close by, would simply take them to the creek and wash them off.

That night was much like the first night. The next day, the old woman Huzi and Eloo came along again. They came after the big Indian had left the tepee. The old woman got down on her knee and held out her hands for the boy. He giggled and after two falls waddled his way over to her. She swung him high into the air as she did a complete spin and he laughed heartily. Martha Jean and Eloo laughed, too.

One thing that Martha Jean noticed was a reverence for the big Indian that brought her here. He was obviously highly respected. Other men sought him out throughout the day and he would listen to them, tell them something and they would nod and walk away. The other thing she noticed was that the tepee where the old woman kept the boy seemed to be the *capitol* of the village. All the time she worked she would continually glance up there to make sure all was well with the boy. Sometimes the woman and little Clay would disappear into the tepee and then come back out after a few minutes. Many times, throughout the day, different people would come to talk with the woman. Always they would walk away with a disappointed look.

During that day, when Huzi brought the child for feeding time, Eloo was able to teach Martha Jean that the name for mother was bii. Then she pointed to Martha Jean and then to the boy and said, "dua", meaning son. Once, Eloo saw Martha Jean watching the big Indian talk with some of the men. She tapped Martha Jean on the shoulder and pointed to the big man.

"Dua." Then she pointed to Huzi, "Bii", she said.

"Alright, my captor is Huzi's son," Martha Jean thought.

To make sure, she went through the pointing and repeating scenario two times. Each time, Eloo nodded and grinned enthusiastically. Then came yet another revelation.

Eloo pointed to the big Indian, then back at herself and said, "Nami". Martha Jean looked at her questioningly. Was Eloo telling her that he was her man? That didn't seem right. Why would he sleep in the same tepee with Martha Jean if they were man and wife? Maybe they weren't married yet. Eloo could see the confusion in Martha Jean's expression. She thought about it for a few seconds and then started again.

She pointed to Huzi and said, "Huzi, Bii" and then to the Indian and said, "Huzi, Dua". Martha Jean had understood this. Huzi was the big man's mother. But what about the relationship between the big man and Eloo? Eloo now pointed to Huzi again and then to herself, "Bii". Now Martha Jean thought she might have it. She pointed to Huzi and then to Eloo, "Bii?" Eloo lit up and with a big grin, vigorously nodded her head.

"Alright, so Huzi is your mother, too. Now I understand, you are his sister."

Eloo was confused at the long sentence but was sure Martha Jean now understood. Now she realized she needed to take one more step.

She pointed at the big man, now walking toward his mother, "Buha", she said.

Buha, what did that mean? Again, Eloo saw the confusion.

She pointed to herself and said, "Eloo."

Then she pointed to Martha Jean and said, "Marta."

Now she pointed back to the man and said, "Buha."

"Ah, now I understand, his *name* is Buha."

Eloo didn't understand the words but she nodded, pointed again at the man and said, "Buha."

A week went by. Nights were always the same. Buha would bring food, they would eat it and he would leave. Sometime during the night, he would return and be there in the morning. Each night after he would leave, she would try to fight back the tears as she thought about Bernie and all their plans and how she wished he were here for her to talk to. He would be able to tell her what to do. Then, she would gather herself together and one more time, resolve to be stronger.

In just one week, her son had learned to walk. She winced as she thought how Bernie would have treasured that accomplishment. Little Clay was still unstable but there was no doubt within a month he would be scampering all around the encampment.

"In a month?" she thought to herself, "My Lord, will we still be here in a month?"

The day was her tenth in the village. A routine of sorts had established itself. She was walking to the stream where she and Eloo would be soaking and stretching a new elk hide.

The scream that pierced the morning air echoed through the little valley. Everyone in sight snapped to see where it came from. It was Huzi! It seemed like everyone in the village ran to the tepee. Martha Jean stayed back, not knowing what her part should be in an emergency. She could see Clay was safe with the other children and needed no help. She continued to work on the hide. It would be over an hour before Eloo came back. Through a few words and signing, and with tear streaked cheeks, she made Martha Jean understand that Great Bear, her father, Buha's father and Huzi's husband, had died.

For the next two weeks, a cloud of gloom hung over the village. Even the children didn't laugh. They played their stick games and tried to catch fish in the stream but they did so quietly without yelling or laughing. It would be a long time before Martha Jean would learn how the burial ceremony took place. She had not been included. One day, Eloo informed Martha Jean that the mourning period was over and that Huzi and Buha had declared that all should now return to normal. And so, it did. At some point it had been declared that Buha was now the official head of the clan. Eloo and Huzi continued to occupy the favored tepee but Buha's tepee was now the *capitol*.

As the months went by she noticed something slowly taking place that she was unsure of. Men, women and children old enough to understand, seemed to treat her with more and more respect. When she asked Eloo about this, Eloo smiled and explained that she was now considered Buha's future wife. Martha Jean was shocked. How could that be? She was white. When she asked about that, Eloo was confused. It became obvious that these people had no sense of bigotry or racial recognition what-so-ever. They had no reason to dislike the white man, or woman, because their mountain retreat had not yet been invaded. It was simple. Buha had lost his wife and he had brought a potential replacement... Maybe. Eloo explained that it would be some time before Buha would make that decision, but Marta would have to agree as well. It was not a forced marriage and Marta would have the option of choosing any other man in the village as well.

1845

"Walking Woman has challenged you!"

Martha Jean had been in the village through two full seasons now, she knew the language and had taught a goodly amount of English to Eloo and Buha. Buha was motivated because he wanted to be able to converse with the white man who seemed to be passing through the lowlands more and more. He was convinced that coexistence with the white men could be had for his people. They just needed to understand the needs of each other.

It was Eloo, "Walking Woman has challenged you!" There was fear in her voice.

"What do you mean, Eloo?" Martha Jean knew who Walking Woman was. By now, she knew everybody in the clan.

"Walking Woman wants my brother to marry her. But she knows he won't as long as you are living with him. She wants to challenge you for your spot in his tepee."

"What kind of challenge?"

"A battle with knives. Until one is dead or leaves the tribe."

69

Neil James

Martha Jean was speechless. She could barely believe what Eloo was telling her. She had noticed that Walking Woman had always been rude to her since the day she arrived. She had asked Eloo about it and Eloo had told her that she had always thought, when Buha finished grieving over the loss of his first wife that he would choose her. That had not happened. Now, Walking Woman could tell that Buha had eyes only for Martha Jean. Martha Jean was shocked. She knew that Buha had adopted her son as his own. He had never shown much in the way of caring for her, though. She guessed he kept her in his tepee only as the mother of his adopted son. They had never once slept under the same robe. He had never once indicated that he wished to sleep under the same robe.

"I can't fight her. I know nothing of that kind of battle."

"You have no choice. You have been challenged. You must fight."

"What if I say no?"

"Then you will be sent out of the village forever and you will never see your son again."

"Would Buha allow that?"

"He will have no choice. It is the law of our tribe. If challenged, you must fight or be sent from the tribe. You will be stripped of your clothes and sent out naked. You will die."

Fear gripped every bit of Martha Jean's being.

"When?"

"At the full moon."

"That's only two weeks away!"

The next morning, instead of leaving the tepee, Buha told her that she would go on the horse with him that day. Bert Morgan's black steed was brought around to his tepee and she climbed into the saddle. Buha was mounted bareback on a big white horse that he regularly rode when hunting. She followed him out of camp for half an hour before he stopped on top of a long flat ridge.

He explained to her in a combination of English and Shoshone that he had no choice but to allow the challenge. He did have a choice on who he hoped would win. It was his intention to spend the days before the full moon on teaching her how to fight with a knife.

"If she wins, will you marry her?"

He looked at her for several seconds before answering.

"When you win, I would like to have you as my woman. As my wife."

She looked into his eyes and saw something she had never seen before. A softness. A vulnerability. What she saw was love.

The strips of buckskin, woven into a rope, were tightly tied around each of their left wrists with about three feet between them. In their right hands were the knives. They stood inside a human circle made up of nearly all the men of the clan. Behind the men, peering in from side to side, to catch glimpses of what was happening, were the women. Martha Jean had worked hard to learn every move, every bit of combat wisdom, every advantage that Buha had tried to teach her during the previous two weeks.

They had spared with sticks. He had told her she was ready. Still, her knife hand was sweaty. The cold, hard eyes of Walking Women showed nothing but confidence and hate. Martha Jean was afraid of dying but equally afraid of killing another person, even if given no choice.

The two stood, crouched over, face to face, waiting for the clan's head man to give the order to start. Buha, hesitating, wishing with all his soul that he didn't have to give that order, finally, with all eyes on the women, closed his own eyes for a long moment, opened them and gave the word.

Instantly, Walking Woman lunged with a sweeping knife stroke. The sharp blade cut across the front of Martha Jean's dress exposing but only scratching her stomach. She sucked in and leapt to her left. Walking Woman recovered instantly and jerked on the rope as she made another straight forward plunge. This time, Martha Jean was ready for it and, turning to her right spun completely around, avoiding the lunge. Walking Woman used the momentum to throw herself backward onto the ground pulling Martha Jean with her. Raising her feet, she caught Martha Jean in the stomach and vaulted her completely over her and onto her back. Walking Woman made a quick roll over and slashed at Martha Jean's neck. The rope was wrapped too tight around Martha Jean's waist and she came up short. Both women jumped to their feet. Martha Jean spun in the opposite direction and came back around with her own knife into Walking Woman's right wrist. Walking Woman screamed and dropped her knife. Without hesitating, Martha Jean, in one move, kicked the knife away and swept her opponent's feet from beneath her. Before Walking Woman even hit the ground on her side, Martha Jean was astraddle her and rolling her onto her back. She quickly wrapped the rope around Walking Woman's neck and yanked on it, pulling the other woman's left arm tightly behind her head. Walking Woman started to strike out with her right hand but stopped in mid-swing. Her hand was being connected to her arm only by a tendon. It just dangled there for a second. Martha Jean brought the blade of the knife to Walking Woman's throat and shaking her long, blonde hair out of her face, looked to Buha. His face was stern as he nodded to her. She knew that meant that it was her choice. The rules were simple and direct. She could kill her adversary, or she could let her live. If she chose the latter, the loser would be driven out of the village. No clothing, nothing on her feet and no survival tools. The loser would be alive but expected to walk out of the village and to her death. Martha Jean raised her knife and in one vicious sweep of its blade, cut the rope, stood up, looked down at Walking Woman for just a moment and walked to her tepee. Buha motioned for two of the women to start the process of stripping Walking Woman of her clothes. She was to be sent out of the village naked, taking nothing with her. They needed not bother, she was already bleeding out and losing consciousness. Thirty minutes later, she was dead.

When Buha walked back into the tepee, he found Martha Jean curled into a ball, shaking with great wracking sobs. He sat down, cross-legged beside her but didn't say anything or touch her. He just waited.

Eventually, the sobs subsided, and she sat up and wiped away the tears. She didn't look at him and didn't speak. They sat there, beside each other for a very long time.

It was then that Martha Jean knew she was truly, deeply in love with this great warrior and that even if a rescue was at hand, she would not go back to the white man's world. She could not make that decision for their son, though. That would have to be determined by the three of them at some distant time.

The ceremony was simple. Eloo and two of the other women had spent much time getting her ready. She wore a newly made buckskin dress and beads made from colorful freshwater snail shells. The dress, extending just below her knees, had frills at its bottom and sleeves. Her hair was long and thick and they combed it over and over so it would sparkle in the sun like gold. One long, blonde braid fell to one side of her face, wrapped in a beaded strand. New, beaded moccasins reached to the bottom of her dress. When she stepped out of their tepee, every single person in the village was there. A vibrant and loud shout of approval erupted. Just in front of the gathering stood Huzi and Buha. Buha looked magnificent! He, too, wore new buckskin. Wonderful new moccasins, full length buckskin pants and a buckskin vest, open to his chest, exposing a breast plate comprised of layer upon layer of beads and quills. His glistening black hair was divided into two braids, tied at the ends with beaded conches. He stood tall with his chin held high, proper for his position in the tribe. His face was staunch, showing his resolve, but that expression changed instantly when he saw his bride to be. A wide grin overtook all other emotion.

To be the bride of an Indian chief was indeed daunting for Martha Jean to think about. She was nervous. But, upon seeing the happy face of her chief, all was good. Better than good. All was wonderful. Martha Jean realized she had never been this happy. At least not since the birth of her son. For the first time ever, she felt complete. She belonged right here, right now, forever!

Huzi reached out to each side of her, taking each of the young people's hands and brought them together in front of her. With a colorful scarf, she wrapped the garment around the two wrists, tying them together, and then raised them high in the air for everyone to see. Another great whoop arose from the crowd and Huzi led the newlyweds to the tepee and held open the flap for them to enter. Another cheer arose as the pair disappeared within. Clay, who had been standing quietly watching all that had happened, stood by Eloo, holding her hand. Huzi took his other hand and the three of them walked away.

At four years old, Clay Brackett was becoming quite good at fishing. He could ride a horse as well as most of the older boys. He could speak both English and Shoshoni. Unlike his mother, his hair was dark brown as Bernie's had been. He wore it loose and long. His eyes were a turquoise blue that seemed to drill into Buha's soul when he listened to instructions. His concentration was remarkable. His observance of nature's ways was far advanced. In his mind, his father was Buha. To Buha, he was his son. They were totally, completely dedicated to each other.

At seven years old, he was hunting with his father every time Buha went out. He could send an arrow as straight as any of the warriors with the exception, perhaps of his friend Bow Shooter. He could wrestle with boys two and three years older and often win. By the time he was fifteen, he was muscular and fast afoot. He could out wrestle any other boy in the village and was not easy even for his father. He had learned the ways of the mountains and its residents, both animal and human. In another year he would be able to earn the right to be called a warrior. Although Chief Buha was always willing to help any of the boys in any way needed to become a warrior, by far, most of his efforts went to his son. Clay, Martha Jean had insisted that he be called by his white name, was loved, respected and admired by not only his father, but by just about everyone in the clan. He was tall for his age. Even though everybody knew he was Buha's adopted son, they couldn't help commenting on the similarity in build and attitude. From the time they were old enough to walk, Clay and two other boys were inseparable. As they grew older, he had nicknamed them Knife Thrower and Bow Shooter because of their expertise with those weapons. The names stuck. Knife Thrower was an expert with his blades, often killing rabbits and birds with a single throw. His father, Coyote Killer, bragged constantly about his son's expertise. Coyote Killer was Buha's second in command and recognized as a great warrior. He had collected many coups. He was deadly in hand to hand fighting and with a knife. He had taught his son everything he knew but now said his son was better with his knife than his father.

Bow Shooter had been shooting arrows since he was three years old. His father had begun teaching him with a tiny bow. Now, he was unequalled in his talent. His father had been lost to a cougar attack when the boy was just 12 years old.

The three boys were now warriors having just survived the demanding and dangerous tests that each young man was required to endure. Some took months or years to make it but nearly all, with the continued training from the older men of the tribe, eventually gained the status. Clay and his friends made it on their first attempt.

The Paiutes had been raiding several of the lower valley Shoshoni villages in the past year, stealing stock and other things while the warriors had been away hunting. During two of these raids, young girls had been stolen. In trying to retrieve the youngsters, six Shoshonis had been killed and several wounded. The Paiutes had been ready for the rescue attempts and had suffered little while holding onto the captives.

No such raids had been made on the Mountain Shoshonis while they spent that summer in the mountains but that was certainly because of Buha's reputation. Also, with some sixty warriors, Buha never left the village unguarded. Hunters went out in groups of twenty at a time. The other warriors stayed at home and awaited their turn. Many of the clans that lived along the river were small. They often got together for hunting, fishing and gathering but lived mainly apart from each other by many miles for lack of enough sustenance to maintain bigger groups. Great Bear, Buha's father, had felt that one bigger family would fare better if high in the mountains where game was more plentiful, and that had been proven true.

It was the first week after leaving the mountains for their winter grounds. The trek from the mountains to the mouth of the Owyhee River at the Snake had been long. They had gone right to work setting up the hogans and tepees for the long months ahead. Things were not as organized as normal and many of the younger children didn't yet know the boundaries for their play. They tended to wander.

The two trappers had been trading with the Paiutes to the North for several weeks. They knew that the tribe's warriors had been raiding Shoshoni villages recently and had taken some girls during those raids. When the trappers happened upon the three mountain people's girls that had wandered down the Snake, they quickly decided to take them as trades to the Paiutes. What they didn't know was that they had taken children from Buha's Clan. The Paiutes ask the girls from which people they came and when they were informed that it was from Buha, they told the trappers to take them away. They did not want to cross paths with the might of the Mountain People. By this time the girls had been missing for three days and there was no doubt that a search party was underway. They also knew the reputation of Buha and his people. In a panic, the trappers took the girls at a rapid pace, west into Nez Perce country in hopes of dumping them there and hence leaving the blame with those people.

The Paiutes sent word to Buha telling him about the attempt to trade the girls and what direction the traders were headed. They said that while they were the clan that had captured the other girls from the lowland Shoshonis, they did not want problems with Buha and made this good faith gesture to avoid his wrath.

Buha sent all but one away with instructions for them to return to the upstream Fisheaters the girls they had taken and raid no more. He didn't wait to see what would happen in that regard but immediately put together a rescue party. Since it was only two trappers, he didn't need a large war party.

When Clay heard of this, he gathered his friends and went quickly to Buha.

"Father," he began, "It is right that we three warriors should be chosen to go now after our sisters."

"You have no knowledge of that land or its people."

"You speak truth Father, but we will have the Paiute to guide us much of the way. Also, I can speak the trapper's language. We are now warriors and we want the warrior way."

Buha gave this thought and decided that his adoptive son was right. It was time to give his newest warriors a chance to prove themselves. A large group of braves were already out searching for the girls but Buha now knew they were searching in the wrong direction. He told the young warriors all he knew from what the Paiutes had told him and, with the remaining Paiute as a guide, sent them on their way. The Paiute would take them to a point where they could cut the trail of the trappers on their western escape.

Clay pushed the mounted group hard. By noon the next day they had found the trail and leaving the guide, began the pursuit.

The trappers hurried as best they could but they were on foot and slowed by the pack mules and the girls. It had taken them two full days to cover the ground that Clay Brackett and his two companions ate up in a matter of hours.

The trappers had finally found the Nez Perce for whom they searched but did not get the greeting they had hoped. As soon as they came across the Nez Perce bunch they had been systematically surrounded. The circle closed in until the Indian's lances were within a foot of the trapper's heads. Five of the natives had dismounted and taken their captive's weapons, bound their hands behind their backs and herded them to the campsite. All the time the trappers did their best to explain, without the proper language, using hand signs, that they had come in search of the Nez Perce, that they wished to trade the girls. Either the Natives didn't understand or, more likely, didn't care. They stripped the men of their clothes and boots and left them only with their hats for cover. The girls were made to sit in a triangular, back to back position. They were not harmed or tied. Two were five years old and one four. They were not inclined to bolt.

Hands and feet bound with grass woven ropes; the trappers sat against a tree with red ants traipsing over their bare bodies. The air was cool, the summer gone and the ants were becoming sluggish but still the trappers would feel the sting of an occasional bite.

The leader of the Nez Perce hunting party took all the packs off one mule and led it out of the immediate camp where he unceremoniously cut its throat. Three more came to hoist it up on a tree limb and within minutes had it dressed out. A fire blazed and parts of the animal were roasting.

One of the Indians pointed to the meat cooking on the spit and then to the two captives and said something that brought great laughter from the rest. He was obviously referring to the roasting of the men.

It was the aroma of the cooking meat that caught the attention of Knife Thrower. The fire had been well concealed but the dusk breeze carried its odor for over half a mile. Clay and Bow Shooter were quick to pick up the smell as well. They slowly followed it until they could make out a bit of flickering light on tree tops just over a small ridge. The trio dismounted and tied their horses. Clay motioned for the other two to stay put while he went for a looksee. When he returned, he described what he found.

They watched, counting the Nez Perce. When it was dark and all asleep, they would make their move. Not knowing if the Nez Perce would be resistant of them taking the girls, they decided simply sneaking them out of the camp made sense. As the hunting party finished eating, they turned their attention to the two trappers.

Four of the Indians went to their captives and began untying them. With the others keeping their weapons pointed at them the men were led to the fire and shoved to the ground. At this point several Nez Perce leapt upon the white men and stretching them out on their backs, held them while their leader began turning long sticks in the fire, heating the ends to red hot. The two captives could see what was coming and struggled, yelled and pleaded. All to no avail.

Coming from three sides, the three rescuers got within thirty feet before one of the girls caught sight of Bow Shooter and excitedly jumped up and happily yelled out for him.

Immediately the Nez Perce not holding the men swung their attention to see what had caused the girl to yell. Bow Shooter retreated enough to be out of sight but the girl had called him by name and even though their languages were different, the leader knew enough to know that someone was lurking just outside of their sight.

Now things had changed and the plan of waiting for darkness was no longer viable. The hunting party leader motioned to four of his bunch to go look where the girl was still excitedly looking. They slowly advanced toward the spot and would have soon been upon Bow Shooter. From the cover on the other side of the camp, Clay gave a war whoop and the four turned quickly and started in that direction. When they got to that edge of the encampment, Knife Thrower gave a throaty yell from his third side position.

Then Bow Shooter yelled, followed immediately by Clay and again by Knife Thrower. They left no doubt that the camp was surrounded. The leader of the Nez Perce was nearly as young as the Shoshoni warriors as were the rest of his hunting party. His first instinct was to put a knife to the throat of the naked white man thinking that the intruders might be there to save the trappers. When that brought no response, he jumped to where the girls were sitting and grabbed the hair of the youngest and put the blade threateningly against her neck.

"Bow Shooter! Kill him!" shouted Clay.

The arrow went straight through the Indian's right eye and partially exited through the back of his head. The Indian and the knife instantly toppled to the ground.

The four holding the trappers let go their grips and leapt for their bows and lances. Five of them fell under the Shoshoni arrows before they had a chance to lift a weapon. Four grabbed cover behind trees as best they could. Hoping they couldn't speak Shoshoni, Clay told his companions to quietly join him at his position where he had a clear view of the copse hiding the Nez Perce, whose backs were against a sheer granite wall. They would not be able to move in any of the other three directions without being seen from Clay's perch above. Suddenly, one of the Nez Perce broke from cover and in a diving, rolling plunge made it to the girls. He picked up the oldest and held her in front of him. By this time both Bow Shooter and Knife Thrower were again near Clay and had no shot at the back of the man. With the girl struggling and screaming, he worked his way back into the tree cover with the other Indians.

Shouting in Nez Perce, they were making their demands. Neither Clay nor his friends could understand the words but the meaning was clear. Back off or we will kill the girl. During all this commotion, the trappers had stayed on their backs. Suddenly, they jumped to their feet and ran past the fire, each grabbing one of the other two girls and disappeared into the brush where their surviving mule and supplies were waiting. They grabbed their long guns and taking the girls onto Nez Perce horses galloped off into the fading light.

As the footfalls faded into the distance, the Nez Perce were again yelling threats.

"I go close with knife. No sound. Stay in shadows," whispered Knife Thrower. He motioned to a brushy side of the stand of thick willows that hid the four Nez Perce. Clay and Bow Shooter nodded. Although they couldn't see the Indians clearly enough for a shot, flashes of movement between branches told the three Shoshonis where the four Nez Perce were standing. They were perhaps ten feet apart watching in every direction. Had they not had the girl, thought Clay, we could get close to them with a charge. But if they ran into the clearing now the one holding the girl might just kill her. In the meantime, he knew, the trappers were taking the other two farther away.

Suddenly the stand of trees seemed to explode and the four Nez Perce came screaming and hollering out three different directions. Two, not knowing that Knife Thrower was just feet away in the brush, ran straight into him. The first was severely slashed across his throat and in one continued motion the knife plunged into the chest of the second.

Knife Thrower yelled out that two were finished. Clay jumped from his position and came down on the one coming directly toward him. The force of the jump from ten feet above knocked the young brave to his knees and Clay rolled to the side. Both were up and facing each other in crouched stance, ready for battle. Clay reached for his knife but found the sheath empty. The other brave saw this and grinned. With his knife in hand he ran to Clay and made a plunging swipe toward his opponent's mid body. Clay jumped back but not far enough. The blade cut through his buckskin shirt and across his breast. Blood flowed and again the Nez Perce grinned as he motioned for Clay to come toward him. Clay circled behind the still glowing firepit. The young Nez Perce held the knife in a stabbing position and came running to catch him. Clay rolled to the ground and grabbing the long stick the leader had been heating for the trappers, braced it against the ground beside him just as the young Nez Perce lunged. The red-hot pointed stick slid deep into his stomach. For just a moment, the young man, impaled on the thing, seemed confused as if not understanding what had happened. First, he kept his attention on Clay and then looked down at the stick. He never made a sound but crumpled to the ground.

While Clay battled, the last remaining Nez Perce was slowly backing out of the clearing still holding the girl in front of him. He had only a knife but when Clay got up and started for him, Bow Shooter came from the other side. The brave, perhaps not more than sixteen himself, realized he had no chance. He looked at Bow Shooter, then to Clay, then to Knife Thrower who had just emerged from the trees. All were advancing on him, slowly

but with determination. He looked at the
bodies of his hunting party. Then, his
shoulders slumped a little and he dropped
the knife and let go of the girl. He looked at
the white man standing with the two
Shoshonis and asked in broken English,
"Who you?"

Clay stepped forward, picked up the
dropped knife and gently pushed the girl off
to the side. "I am Clay. We come from Buha."

The eyes of the Nez Perce widened in
wonder and then filled with fear.

"Buha? Buha! We know of him. He is
warrior god!"

The young man dropped to his knees
and began to sing a death song. Clay put the
dropped knife to the kneeling boy's throat.
Bow Shooter touched his arm and when Clay
looked at him, he shook his head. Clay
nodded and pulled the knife back. The three
young warriors and the girl watched and
listened for just a moment before walking to
their horses. With the girl on one of the Nez
Perce horses they started after the trappers.
They could hear the death song still being
sung long after they left the camp.

"Perhaps we should have killed him," said Clay.

"Perhaps," said Knife Thrower, "but now he will tell of Buha and more will know of his greatness. Few will be wanting to risk an attack on a *warrior god*." Clay nodded and they all smiled. They knew Buha had a reputation. But *warrior god*? He was just Buha to them. Their teacher and mentor. The man who wrestled with them and laughed with them and played silly jokes on them. His wisdom and proficiency were without question. But still, he was just Buha. While legends are being made, the ones closest to them rarely know it is happening.

Onward hurried the trappers. They rode hard without even stopping for clothing. Hour after hour. The horses were lathered and heaving. They were in wooded mountains with heavy undergrowth and the horses' footing was uneven at the full run forced by the trappers. At length the lead horse stumbled having caught a leg between two fallen trees. The animal fell head over heels forward, the trapper and the girl thrown into the undergrowth. Both were scratched but neither were badly hurt. He yelled at his partner as the man rushed by on his horse. The horseman didn't even slow. He yelled back, "Leave her and hurry behind. I'll see you up ahead!"

The trapper yelled some more but the fading sound of the horse crashing forward was all he could hear. He went to his own horse. The animal stood up but his right front leg just dangled from the knee.

The trapper took a quick look at the girl and began running after his counterpart. The girl sat down on a log some feet away and watched the horse in its agony. Tears rolled down her cheeks. She could do nothing for the animal. She would stay there for over two hours before she heard other horses coming from behind. It was her rescue party.

Knife Thrower and the first girl stayed with the youngster while Bow Shooter and Clay continued on the chase. They found the other girl wandering back from which she came. She had been tossed from the horse and had a sprained wrist along with bruises and scratches. Nothing appeared to be broken. They helped her onto Bow Shooter's horse and the two started back to where Knife Thrower and the other girls waited.

Clay had gone nearly a mile when he spotted movement ahead. As he got closer, he could make out a lone trapper. He was sitting on a log, his head down and his arms dangling to either side. Clay was within thirty yards before the man jerked his head up and looked back down the trail. Seeing Clay, he jumped up and began to scramble up the hillside. He reached a rim rock some fifty feet above and began to scale it. Clay halted his horse near where the man had been sitting. He notched an arrow and started to pull back the bow string when the man lost his footing and came tumbling back down the steep hillside. He stopped rolling about ten feet from Clay and immediately jumped to his feet. He looked at Clay and began to beg. He spoke in French and Clay couldn't make out the words.

"If you want to beg for your life you should do it in English or Shoshoni," Clay said quietly.

"Yes, English! I speak good English. Please, it wasn't my idea to take the girls. It was Jacque! He is a very bad man! Let me go and I will help you catch him."

Clay looked at him for a few seconds as if considering what to do.

"No, I do not think so."

In less than a second the bow came up, the tension stretched and released and the arrow plunged into the man's heart. Clay watched as he fell and then rode on.

It was near dark when Clay came to the dead horse. It had been ridden into the ground by the other trapper. The torn up surrounding brush and dirt showed the animal had thrashed about for a long time before finally succumbing. The trapper hadn't even taken the few seconds needed to put the animal out of its misery. Clay spat.

"You will be revenged my brother."

It was getting dark but the trail was easy to follow now and he kept on. He stopped to look ahead with the light from a full moon. The trail started up a steep rise ahead that led into a crevice with sheer walls on each side. It was evident that area Indians had been using the narrow passage for long times past. He looked around for possible alternative routes but saw no options. He dismounted and began cautiously leading forward and up. As the walls closed in, the way ahead leveled out and he could see that the path began a downward slope at the other end. The sound of the horse's footfalls echoed as the pair made their way. Clay stopped often to look and listen. With the moon's light barely penetrating the trench ahead the darkness was nearly complete. He could see only slight detail of the path and just the horse's breathing made it to his ears.

It was another two hundred feet before the channel opened up. He took one more look and then mounted the horse and charged forward in a full gallop, hoping to make it through without being much of a target. The shot hit the horse in the head and it dropped instantly from beneath its rider. Clay leapt from its back but was catapulted into the wall. He was dazed and the wind knocked out of him. The next shot came from atop the rim and sent shards of granite spitting at him and stinging his face, narrowly missing his eyes. When he tried to move, he found his leg caught beneath the dead horse. He looked for his bow but couldn't see it. His knife was not in its sheath but he could see it laying near the horse's head. He stretched and tried to reach it. A foot too far from his fingers. He could hear the shooter making his way down the far slope of the crevice as he continued trying to free his leg. He could move it a little but couldn't get it to pull free. The pain was intense and he wondered if it was broken. A movement caught his attention and he could see the silhouette of a man near the opening of the chink coming slowly his way.

The trapper surveyed the situation as he got close enough. He lit a match and held it near to Clay's face.

The Frenchman jumped back in astonishment and in broken English said, "White man! Not Indian. Why you follow me?"

"You took those girls from the tribe that raised me. Now you will die for doing that."

The trapper laughed a nervous chuckle and said, "I will die? Me? I have the gun. You stuck under the horse and have no weapon. You are just a child. Still you say it is me that will die? No, I don't think so Indian boy. I think I kill you pretty much quick."

He struck another match so he could again look at Clay Brackett to make sure he was really white. He leaned over the horse to check for some kind of weapon that he might have missed. Seeing none he took the butt of his long gun and slammed it down on Clay's trapped leg. When no sound or flinch came from the boy, he raised it again.

"Maybe so you feel it this time?"

In the dark he didn't notice Clay picking up the piece of slag. With all his might, Clay slung the thing at the man's head and heard the thud. At the same time, he launched as far forward as he could. Just enough to get his hand on the rifle as it fell from the trapper's hand.

The trapper was sprawled out over the rump of the horse, unmoving. For the next half an hour, Clay used a rock to dig beneath his captured leg. Constantly keeping an eye on the lump of the trapper. Finally, inch by inch, he pulled his leg from under the beast.

It took another ten minutes for the blood flow to return. He winced as the accompanying pain came with the circulation. Finally, he used the gun as a crutch and regained his footing. The moon had made its way far enough in the sky to now shine into the narrow passageway. He took the powder horn and beaver skin pouch of balls from around the trapper's neck and pulled the riding blanket from the dead horse. It took some looking in the dim light but he was able to find his bow, arrows and knife. As he put the quiver and bow over his head and shoulder, he walked back toward the trapper who was just coming awake.

"Damn you, boy. I will get you now."

He got to his knees just as Clay walked by.

"I gonna kill..."

He didn't say more because without even looking down or breaking stride, Clay had swiped the knife under the man's chin, cutting his throat. Clay Brackett heard the gurgling sound but never looked back as he started his hike toward home. At sixteen years of age, he had already killed more men than most of the much older warriors in his clan would in a lifetime. He felt nothing of that though. He just felt tired and his leg hurt.

Neil James

PART TWO

1843

   Bert Morgan had been left for dead
when the wagon train was attacked by the
Warm Springs Indians those many years
earlier. Fact was, he should have been dead.
Most other men would have been. He had
two arrows in him and had been clubbed for
good measure.   One of the attackers,
checking for any that might have survived,
had kicked him for a sign of life but getting
no response had moved on. The wagons had
been burned, the livestock and anything the
Indians found of value, had been taken.

There was little left sparing the dead pilgrims.

Bert Morgan lay on his back well into the next afternoon before something deep inside brought him back from the brink. Slowly, painfully, he opened his eyes to the bright sunshine. His head had been bashed on the left side leaving a gash. The bleeding had coagulated and now there was a crust of dried blood. As he started to move, the arrows made their presence known. The pain almost made him pass out again. One was lodged in his left side, while the other was in his chest. He felt around the one in his chest and could feel the arrowhead. It had hit a rib and broken off at an angle and lay flat just beneath the skin. Through some quirk, the wooden shaft still stuck up making it look like the arrow was deeply embedded. With some effort, he simply gave a yank on the shaft and let it fall aside. The arrowhead stayed under the skin. His head swam with the pain and nausea swept over him. He lay still for a long time. He had drifted off to sleep only to be awakened by the flapping wings of the vultures that had begun to gather for the feast. That realization helped him garner the will to continue. He had a hard time making his arms reach to the arrow in his side but was finally able to discover that it had gone through the fleshy part of his side and the actual arrowhead was in the ground. He would have to break off the feathered end of the arrow and pull the rest of the shaft through the back side. He took a deep breath that hurt all over and forced his body onto its side. With one slight move at a time he got to his knees and then, trying desperately to hold onto consciousness, crawled to the nearest wagon. He rose to his feet using the wagon wheel for support. After several minutes of trying to stop the spinning in his head, he stumbled to the bank of the Snake River and gingerly washed the blood from his injured head and face and the grime from his hands. The arrow still stuck out the front and back of his side. The pain he felt when he touched it made him dizzy. His head was throbbing. He sat down on the bank to muster his determination and rested for a good half an hour. He tried to envision how he might stop the bleeding once he withdrew the arrow. It would be gushing both front and back. He hauled himself to his feet and stumbled like he was drunk back to the wagons, or what was left of them. There was not a thing left in any of them that had not been burned. He had to get that arrow out and stave the bleeding from the chest wound as well, though it seemed to be clotting on its own to some degree.

Through all of this he tried not to look at the bodies of his charges. The people that had trusted him to get them safely through to Oregon. He had failed them grievously. He couldn't help glancing at them as his hoarse voice swore at the gathering vultures. He wiped at tears rolling down his face as he saw a young mother still holding her baby. She had died trying to protect the infant but the arrow that had killed her had gone all the way through and into the child as well. He staggered to the wheel of one of the wagons and leaned heavily on it. He thought he might throw up. He reached up to wipe away the tears so he could see but raising his hand beyond his neck caused too much pain. His hand came to rest on his kerchief. He had forgotten about it. It would work to plug one of the holes when he pulled out the arrow. He pulled it from his neck and stuffed it into his pants pocket. Looking down, he saw one of his outriders lying on the ground a few feet away. With great effort he made it to him and almost collapsed as he leaned over and removed the man's kerchief from his body.

"Sorry Sam, you was a good man." He grunted, "I reckon you might not mind me using your hanky."

He stumbled back to the river and tried to sit down on the bank. His foot slipped on the mud and he went sliding feet first on his tail end. Now he was knee deep in the slowly flowing water. He gathered himself and washed out the two bandanas. He pulled open his shirt just enough to see the hole left by the embedded arrowhead. Looking at it made him woozy, but he could see, for now at least, the bleeding had stopped.

Pulling himself back up on the bank he desperately wanted to lie down and rest, but first that arrow had to be dealt with. He reached into his pocket and pulled out the now wet, and reasonably clean, kerchiefs.

Reaching down, he was surprised to find that his knife was still in its sheath inside his boot. How had the raiders missed it?

He pulled it out and began to work at cutting through the arrow shaft as close to his skin as he could. The pain of the slight movement was searing. After some effort, the feathered shaft fell away. Now, if he could get a decent purchase on the arrowhead, he could, he hoped, pull it through and out in one singular motion. He slumped down on his opposite side in the grass near the riverbank. He was well aware that he might pass out when he made the extraction. He picked up a piece of wood the size of his thumb and gripped it in his teeth. He placed one of the bandanas over the cut off end of the arrow and with one hand, held the other where the shaft exited his back. Then, taking a deep breath, with the other hand tightly gripping the arrow, he jerked with all his waning strength. The pain hit like a torch. He knew he gave forth a muddled yell but was surprised to find that he had also bitten through the wood. He desperately tried to press the bandanas over the holes.

He thought he was going to go unconscious but was able to hold on, even though his vision blurred and spun. How long he laid there he didn't know but it was getting dark when he finally managed to move. Although the kerchiefs were soaked through, he felt like the bleeding could be subsiding some.

After watching the stars grow brighter and brighter in the magnificent Idaho sky, he drifted off to sleep. He was awakened by the howl of a coyote just a hundred feet away. Far to the northeast, he could see a slight greyness in the sky above the other mountain range sixty miles away. He was stiff and hurt everywhere. He had rolled onto the side of the arrow sometime during the night. That was probably a good thing since the grass on the ground held the kerchief against the wound. He tested his body just enough to know he could sit up. It hurt. The wounds in his chest and side were agonizing with each breath. His head still had an edge to it, but the throbbing had subsided somewhat.

"Well, old boy, I think I just might beat you again." He talked to Death as if an old adversary, as it had been several times in his life.

Slowly, ever so slowly, he gained his feet. He was some unstable, but he was upright. Barring infection, which was no given, he thought he might make it. But make it to where? He had no horse, he was badly wounded, and he had no food. He did have plenty of water and for that he was thankful. He was cold, he was shivering. He needed to build a fire. That would not be a problem. The hardwood floors of several of the wagons were still smoldering after these... what? Hours? Days? He wasn't sure. The sideboards were gone but the flooring was still held in place by the metal framework. He picked up some dry grass and some sticks and piled them on the smoking floorboards. It took only seconds for the grass to burst into flames. He stood close and added branches. Soon, he had a flame shooting into the starlit sky above. He warmed himself and continued to add branches.

As dawn broke and he could see around the scene of destruction, he surveyed the bodies. Vultures erupted into flight and coyotes moved warily to a safe distance to watch. He walked to Sam's corpse and offered thanks one more time as he stripped the man's belt. With his knife he cut off a long piece of a woman's petticoat that had evidently been discarded by the Indian raiders. He wondered to himself why he hadn't seen it the day before. He struggled out of his blood-soaked shirt and wrapped the cloth around his wounds. He ushered a grim smile as he found that they were lined up perfectly and one bandage would suffice for all three of his punctures. He used the belt of his friend to hold them in place. The shirt he washed out in the river as best he could and hung it close to the fire to dry. It had holes in it but so did all the other shirts around the burned-out wagons and of course, so did he. The sun was just up in the northeast. He decided that he needed to survey the entire area. And then it hit him, what if there were more survivors? What if all were not dead? How could he have been so selfish as to not check each and every soul lying scattered about? He began slowly, because he could only move slowly, to check each one. He counted as he did so. He said each name reverently as he identified every one of the folks he had come to know so well. All gone, everyone dead. The heat of each day had made the bodies swell and he thought that he had to bury them. He found a pick and shovel that had been overlooked by the Indians. He didn't have the strength yet to dig but he would as soon as he possibly could. He was contemplating this when a thought suddenly slipped into his aching head.

Out loud he said to himself, "Wait, there were eight women and two infants."

He realized he had found just seven women and one infant. The Brackett woman and her baby! He hadn't found them! When he got his strength back just a bit, he made another tour of the site. They were not to be found. Then he remembered her husband had been down by the river and she had taken the baby to be near him. It was just a quick glance at the time but now he remembered it well. She might have gotten away. More likely, she had been taken captive. His heart quickened. He would have to find her. He would have to rescue that woman and child.

That was the last thought he had before the loss of blood overtook him and everything started to close in on him with a swirl of darkness. He was able to lower himself to the ground and lie down before consciousness left him.

He awoke to something cold and wet on his face. Something was swaying and shaking the ground and his wounds hurt from it. With effort he removed a wet cloth that covered his face and opened his eyes, quickly closing them against the bright sun. He raised one hand for shade and tried again.

"Well sir! Welcome back to the living."

It took a moment to focus but when he did, he could see a young man with a big mustache and smile. He realized the shaking was not the ground but a wagon moving along at a slow pace. He was swinging back and forth in a makeshift hammock strung from cross members of a covered wagon. The canvas had been pulled back so that it covered just half the box.

It took a minute to get his wits about him. The young man beside him had seen him wince and pulled the canvas just enough to offer some shade.

Morgan mustered what strength he could and was able to croak out, "Water."

A canteen came to his parched lips and he drank until he heard the voice caution against over doing it.

"Where am I?"

"You're safe in a military wagon."

That was it until he found himself going through the same awakening routine again. He wasn't sure if he had passed out or had drifted off to sleep. He must have been out for quite a while because when he tried to carry on the conversation it was a different face that looked questioningly down on him. The bright sun had been replaced with darkening clouds.

"Thanks, mind filling me in on what I missed?"

"Sir?"

"I guess I've been out for a while. What have I missed?"

This young soldier was clean shaven and red hair poked out from beneath his cap. He held the canteen to Morgan's lips as he began his reply.

"You bet, my name is Corporal Jonathan Leggett and I'm with the United States Army 1st Dragoons headed for the mouth of the Columbia River. We came across what was left of your wagon train and found that you were the only one still alive. We patched you up as best we could and buried the others. That was four days ago."

Bert pushed away the canteen and adjusted his position to take some pressure off his side wound. "Four days ago? Where are we now?"

"Well, I can't rightly tell you specific like. We're still following the Snake River and heading in a Northwesterly direction. Kinda like you were doin' I suspect. Lieutenant says we should have another few days before we reach the Columbia and head for the coast. The Pacific Ocean coast. You ever seen the ocean, sir?"

"Just once," he winced from the pain, "I was the wagon master on that train back yonder. I scouted for another one to within a hundred miles of the ocean a couple years back and figured I might as well take the opportunity to jaunt on over there and have me a looksee. Figured I might never get another chance. Purdy impressive. Give me another swig, will ya?"

The boy reached behind him and handed over the canteen.

"I ain't never seen it but I hear as to how it is something to behold. I look forward to it. Given as to how you ain't gonna be healed up anytime soon and there ain't no where's else in between to git yerself back into one piece, well sir, I reckon as to how you might be seein' it agin. Right alongside me."

"What about Fort Boise. Did we stop there?"

"Oh, yes sir. There was some talk of leavin' ya there to heal up but they had no doctor and we do and they just decided it'd be best to keep you with us."

Morgan nodded slightly and closing his eyes, drifted back off to sleep.

As the five wagons and thirty mounted troops made their way along, the lieutenant, having no one, including himself that had ever made the trip, called upon Bert often to give guidance as to the best route. More than once, the lieutenant admitted that he would have taken the wrong direction. Bert had suggested taking a much shorter route that he knew through the Blue Mountains but Josh, the lieutenant, had reluctantly followed his written orders which dictated that the soldiers follow the route demanded by less than competent superiors. Those orders stated that he would follow the Snake to the Columbia and hence to the mouth of the great river.

The weeks that followed allowed Morgan to regain some of his strength. It took more than a month to reach the mouth of the Columbia and two more weeks at the camp on the coast before he was able to travel on his own. Already the troops had built three log structures and erected two large tents of canvas. Corrals had been put together and the livestock secured. Their mission was to protect that part of the region from British troops that were still trying to claim portions of the territory. The tenth

President of the United States, John Tyler, and his congress, felt strongly that the United States owned that same territory and were willing to defend it. More troops would arrive within the next several months, but the young lieutenant's small force was the forward guard.

When Bert finally felt he was ready to depart, against the advice of the company's corpsman, the lieutenant cut out a good strong horse, and a steady pack mule, along with the rigging necessary for travel. Bert was at least as well-equipped as any horse soldier at the camp. Probably better.

"Bert, I don't rightly know how to pay ya back for all you done for this outfit," said Lieutenant Josh Braxton. They were standing on the wooden deck attached to the front of the officer's tent looking out on the waves of the Columbia lapping the gently sloping bank. To the west about half a mile this great stream emptied into the Pacific.

Braxton continued, "This here nag and the worthless mule might get a start on it though. Sure wish you could stay with us."

"Well, Josh, this nag as you call it is probably the best mount you coulda found for me in your whole bunch and I happen to know this mule is the best of the string. I feel guilty ridin' off with em' but somehow I guess I'll live with it." He grinned and Braxton chuckled.

With that the two shook hands and Bert mounted up.

As he gathered the reins the lieutenant said, "Well, ya stay safe out there now and don't be donatin' any of that mane of yourn to no young buck's bragging pole, ya hear?"

"That's my plan. You keep clear of them redcoats."

"Oh, don't worry none 'bout them water rats, we beat em ever time they show their little ratty noses. They ain't been much since Washington ran em out of New York Harbor fifty years past."

Bert nodded, smiled, tipped his hat and rode away without looking back. He gave a wave to the little fort's outer guard as he spoke quietly to the spunky horse and leaned ever so slightly forward. The animal responded instantly into a singlefoot gait.

That smooth and comfortable pace rarely found in horses has always been considered a treat to any rider and highly prized. The mule didn't pick up quite as quickly but soon followed forth. The jingling of the animal's pack told Bert that he was still back there.

That first night, some thirty miles up the Columbia found the animals grazing on good grass and an exhausted Bert Morgan wishing he had listened to the corpsman that told him he was going to feel the objection of his not yet healed wounds. That young man of medicine knew his stuff and Bert felt every bit of the soldier's wisdom. He hurt everywhere.

Several days and nights later the pains of the days' travel began to ease and he was feeling more his old self.

"Old is the right," he thought aloud. He still considered himself a younger man, but his body had continuously told him something different. By two weeks on the trail the wounds had healed enough to issue forth no pain. Or maybe Morgan had just convinced himself to ignore it. At any rate, he believed himself fully recovered. Rather than follow the Columbia all the way to the

Snake he had instead cut at least a hundred hard miles off by taking across and through the Blue Mountains.

Sixteen days and he had found the Snake and was well along its western bank headed south. He had not seen any sign of another human being since waving goodbye to the guard at the fort. By now he was relaxed and not as alert as he should have been. The war whoop snapped him to attention as he looked for its source. There they were! Two hundred feet above him on the rim rock. An arrow and then another and another glancing off the rocks through which he rode. A quick analysis told him that the four warriors above him had no apparent way down to him. The cliff was shear for fifty feet and then loose shale down to the scree he was working his way through. He also decided they had no guns, or they would have been using them. This was most likely a hunting party of young Nez Perce warriors. But young didn't mean they weren't deadly. If they were indeed Nez Perce, they would be well mounted for the tribe boasted the largest number of horses anywhere in the country.

They were known for selectively breeding some of the best horses known to man. He could only hope they couldn't find a way down into the riverbed before he could work his way out of range.

He didn't want to shoot at them for fear the blast that would echo back through the canyon would bring even more of the hostiles. He knew well that they fished the Snake for its salmon and other species but had hoped they wouldn't be there this time of year. He had chosen to make his way through a portion of the deep gorge that would become known as Hells Canyon, deeper in spots even than the Grand Canyon, in order to avoid them. It had gone well up until that first arrow. He was at the point up the river where the canyon was beginning to become wider and shallower. The going had been slow as he often had to swim the horse and mule because the cliffs rose from the water itself. At one point, he was forced to swim across to open space and then return as the land again disappeared into the water.

The arrows had stopped. He didn't know if they were running low or if they knew of a place where they could intercept him farther upriver. Still, they were following above, looking down at him and moving along as he moved. At a sheer cliff that jutted into the river, he once again was forced into the water although it was not deep enough to force him to swim the animals. He stayed in the saddle and was dismayed by what he saw as he rounded the monolith.

Less than a quarter mile beyond, the canyon widened out into a gradual slope on both sides of the river. On the west side, his side, he could make out at least eight mounted men sitting their horses in a side-by-side line. They were looking directly at him. He couldn't make out much detail, but he had no doubt that they were Nez Perce. He sat there for a minute trying to decide what to do. Four more horses came from above to join the others. That would be the ones that had been harassing him from the cliffs. Then the line began slowly advancing. He waited and watched. He wanted to be sure what or who he was up against. He had three choices as he saw it. He could swim across the river and try to outrun them but that didn't seem much of a choice as they weren't burdened with a mule and would probably reach the other side before he could. At this point, he wasn't willing to give up the mule.

Another choice was to wait until they were closer and then start shooting at them and possibly open enough of a hole in the line that he could just plow through. Again, with the mule in tow that didn't seem much of an idea either.

The third option seemed best. Wait until he could see how they were armed and go back around the rock wall from which he had just come. If they didn't have guns, they would have a hard time picking him off as he retreated. Timing would be everything. If he saw long guns, he would have to abandon the mule and just run for his life. If not, he just might make it through the inevitable onslaught of arrows and out of their sight. Still, they would be following even if he made it. This would not be over by a long shot.

Into a trot and then a gallop they came. He stood his ground, rifle in hand. Then he could see the leader well enough to know he carried only a bow. Time to go! He turned the horse and with the reluctant mule splashed back into the water. Arrows dropped around him, kerplunking into the water and he heard one hit something on the mule. Then suddenly, the shafts stopped falling and looking back the pursuers couldn't be seen, blocked by the rock pillar.

Now he had another choice to make. It would take them maybe three or four minutes for the first one to come into sight around the hundred-foot-high sheer rock outcropping. He could try to make a run for it, or he could do the other. That was it. Just ahead some thirty yards was large scree that came to the water. These boulders were five to ten feet high. There was no way through it, but wading in less than a foot of water, would allow the way around it. On the other side he could conceal the horse and mule and take up a perfect line of defense. He quickly made his way into the shallow water and behind the huge boulders. He ground tied the animals by rolling a couple large watermelon sized rocks onto their lead-ropes and began laying out his weaponry. He had two revolvers and his long gun. He would get just one shot with the long gun before having to reload. He would need to choose his target well and be accurate. The handguns would have to wait until the charge was within forty feet. The odds were not good, but they were the only odds he had.

Set up between two of the five-foot-high boulders he had his rifle already aimed at the place he had decided was where he would take the long gun shot.

That would be at the leader. He didn't know how Nez Perce handled losing their main man, but some tribes of the plains would lose all enthusiasm for fighting if their leader fell. He hoped that would be the case with the Nez Perce.

They came then, slowly, cautiously around the stone wall. The leader first. A big man. Maybe in his thirties. Clad in Mexican peasant clothes with a buckskin cord tied around his waist and wearing moccasins. A flat brimmed hat with one feather in the band topped his long black hair. Strings of beads rested on his chest. Seashell earrings hung on each side of his stern face. Sitting bareback on his spotted horse that the tribe had become so well known for, he did look magnificent. He stopped exactly where the rifle was pointed and surveyed the trail before him. He couldn't have seen anything of his prey excepting the round hole in the barrel of the rifle that was pointed at him. He didn't see it. He turned to watch as the rest of his band came out of the water and onto the bank behind him. He turned back toward Morgan's hiding place and motioned for the group to move forward. That's when Bert pulled the trigger. The man's face disintegrated, and he plummeted to the ground. Three rapid shots from his first revolver and three more tumbled to the sandy beach amid screams and confusion. Four were dead before they could find the source of the shots. Three more charged toward Bert's cover while two started to retreat back around the rock face. Bert took careful aim and shot them both in the back. He didn't want them waiting for him should he survive this skirmish. Three had dismounted and were scrambling for what scarce cover they could find at the base of the cliff. One of the charging three wheeled his horse into the water and came around where he could see Bert. His bow was fully pulled, and the arrow released and missed before the bullet knocked him into the river. He began to float downstream.

Bert Morgan had been through this kind of battle before and was on automatic. No time for fear. No time for panic. Just execute. Turning back to the other two warriors coming fast at him he shot one at just ten feet away and pulled the trigger on the other one. The first revolver was empty and the second one didn't fire. Misfire? Empty? Didn't matter. The warrior was leaping from his horse onto the boulder that had concealed Morgan. Bert dropped the gun and picked up the skinning knife that he had laid out beside him. The short stocky Indian let out a whoop as he let fly an arrow that missed by inches, pulled his knife and flew off the rock onto Morgan's waiting knife. His weight took Morgan to the ground. Even though the knife was embedded deep in his chest, the man still had fight left in him and he pushed away and tried to take a weak

swing at Bert with his knife. Bert blocked the
swipe, wrenched the knife loose and used it
to cut the warrior's throat. The remaining
warriors were probably three of the young
four that had originally discovered him. He
hoped they would stay hidden long enough
for him to reload. The skirmish made his
wounds hurt and it was a struggle to stand.

Keeping his eyes on the small sheltered
area that concealed the three young warriors,
he began reloading by touch. He wanted the
revolvers loaded first because the Indians
were so close, he thought the rifle would be
too awkward. He could hear a heated debate
going on among the three as he finished
loading. He could also tell they were scared.

"Hey! Come on outta there. I'll let you
go on down river afoot. Otherwise, I'm
agonna kill all three of ya."

He was sure they couldn't understand
what he was yelling at them but he didn't
speak their language, so it was the best he
had to offer. He expected no response and
got none. He could hear more conversation.
Voices rising and lowering but always with
fear. He sat watching the spot for another 15

minutes with no change. He knew they still had bows and arrows and could probably throw knives as well. He wasn't about to go back down river but couldn't figure how to get past these braves without being shot.

"You no Keel?"

Morgan jumped from his sitting position not knowing if he really heard what he thought he heard.

"No kill," he shouted back.

"We go far down reever?"

"Yes, far down river."

"You no Keel?"

"No kill," shouted back Morgan.

He waited. Then six hands raised above the shelter. Three bows were displayed but no arrows were notched. After another thirty seconds, heads, shoulders and finally torsos appeared. He had been right. The three were probably no more than sixteen years old and were obviously scared half to death. Morgan climbed to the top of the rock in front of him holding a revolver in each hand. All three shrank back some but he motioned for them to walk out to the river and around him. They began to move without taking their eyes from him. The one in the lead tripped over the dead body of one of the braves but caught himself before he fell. The other two quickly walked around the corpse. Now they began to take in the other dead and more fear began to show. At the riverbank they started to walk upstream until Morgan yelled at them and motioned for them to turn around and head the other way, down river. The first one nodded and complied. The other two followed. The warrior that had ridden around the boulders and shot an arrow at Morgan had floated away but his horse obediently stood where it had stopped. As the last boy in line walked by it he nonchalantly reached for the braided hackamore.

"No ya don't," said Morgan.

The boy looked at him, dropped the braid and walked on leaving the horse standing in place.

Morgan watched as the boys picked their way down through and around boulders until they were nearly half a mile away. Then he went to inspect the bodies. All were dead or almost so. He thought he should finish off the two that were nearly gone but something in him wouldn't let him do it. Instead he got his coffee cup from the mule, scooped up some water and gave both a drink. Neither were strong enough to lift a hand and besides, all the fight was gone from them. He pulled both into a sitting position, leaning against a boulder within two feet of the lapping water, side by side. They both looked at him but didn't try to speak. He gathered the only three head of horses that hadn't run off and tethered them where the wounded Indians could see them and close enough to the water that the animals could drink. With that he took one final look down stream and could just make out three spots moving slowly away.

"Good boys," he said as he swung into the saddle, pulled the mule's lead-rope free of the rock that held it in place and once again rode around the gigantic protruding wall of granite.

Late on an overcast afternoon, nineteen days after leaving the west coast, he rode up to the burned-out wagons. They were all still there just as he had left them. He tied his horse to a wagon wheel and walked another twenty yards to a spot by the riverbank where twenty-eight graves rested. Each grave was marked with a cross made of tree branches. The soldiers had done all they could to leave a respectable little cemetery. Except for the much smaller graves of the children, Bert had no idea which grave was which. During his days convalescing, he had carved out the names of each member of the train on a board. He had carried it all this way atop the camping gear on the mule. With some effort he used the back of his knife to pull out nails from one of the wagons and then cut off an unburned piece of a doubletree to use as an upright. The name-board was nailed to the piece and in one of the graves where the covering dirt was still soft, he drove it into the ground. At least for now, until it rotted away, the names of these people, friends really, would be known to any, if any, that might pass by. He thought that if he could make it work, that he would someday get a stone marker with the names. That would have to wait for now. He stood gazing at the graves, hat in hand, for several minutes. Then he looked back toward the mountains to the southwest. Too much time had gone by for him to track the Brackett woman and her baby. He rode a wide half circle anyway, just in case. Too many old tracks. There had been too many in the war party and it appeared that they had broken off in three different groups when they left. Two of the groups had evidently crossed the river and headed back down river. One had stayed along the bank on his side. It appeared that all were headed for home to the north. There was no way of knowing if the woman was with any of them. He swore a bit and pulled his hat down tight over his eyes and gave the willing horse a touch of his spurs. He headed back up the river and on to Missouri.

Bert Morgan was through with wagon trains. Never again, he vowed, would he be a part of taking people into that kind of danger. He had his fill of watching people die from diphtheria, cholera and dysentery. He had lost animals to Indian raids in the past, but his planning and expertise had kept his fellow travelers free of loss. Not until this raid had he ever felt that devastation. The difference was simple. Always before, he had been part of large trains, the ones able to pay a wagon master. Usually of a hundred or more wagons. This time, he had agreed to be captain of such a small group because he intended on settling in the west himself. One of the wagons that had burned had been his. The venture had obviously been a mistake.

His vision of taking up a place of his own in the Oregon country hadn't been his own. Well, not initially anyway. Bert Morgan had been in love only once in his life. It had happened while scouting for a previous train. A city of rolling houses that took months to arrive at their destination. Along the way he had met Ellen. Ellen Elaine Riggins. Nineteen years old and smart and mature beyond her years. Irish with a deep accent that tickled Morgan half to death. She traveled with a preacher's family arranged for by her employer. She was being sent to the Yamhill District of the Oregon coast to work for the Hudson Bay company who were trying to recruit young women in hopes of establishing families to settle the area. Of course, the ladies only knew that there would be adventure and work. The pay, they were told would be good and if, for any reason they were unhappy after a years' service, they would happily be returned to their place of origin at no cost.

The preacher's family became concerned as she obviously fell head over heels for Morgan. They also realized Morgan was just as infatuated.

Ellen didn't share their concerns. She knew the man she loved had always been a loner. She knew he took no slight or aggression from any man without retribution, but she also felt that there was something inside the man that would put her and their family first when settled down. Before the end of the journey, they were married.

When the destination of the train had been achieved, she hugged and kissed the family members goodbye and with her whole future shining bright with the morning sun, rode side by side with her new husband. They would go back to Philadelphia where Bert was sure he could work with his brother-in-law in his wagon building business. It would be a confining and probably boring work, but he would have his life with Ellen and a family to make it worthwhile.

The long ride back east was a wonderful honeymoon and the weeks of making plans for the return trip and a start of a new life was beyond exciting. For the first time in his life, Bert Morgan could see a way out of his life of fighting. With Ellen, he knew who he *could* be.

When she died, he wasn't there. They were not yet close to their destination and had stopped for a few days' rest. He had been gone on some unremembered business that didn't even need to happen. When he returned and walked through the door of their hotel room the town's doctor was just leaving. The wife of the hotel owner sat on the bed next to her.

"I'm sorry." The doctor shook his head sadly and said, "She developed a fever yesterday and I couldn't get it under control.

She passed just a few minutes ago. I wish I could tell you what caused it. I just don't know." He touched Morgan's shoulder and again said, "I'm sorry."

The woman stood up and walked to the door. With genuine sympathy she said, "Let me know when you are ready, and I'll send up the undertaker."

That had been over two years ago but it seemed like yesterday in many ways. He spent that winter living in the same hotel but a different room. On many nights he had to be carried to his room after drinking himself unconscious. He got into fights with men that had no quarrel with him just to let out some of the pain.

Finally, sitting once again in the town's jail cell, mostly sober from the night before, he accepted a cup of coffee from the constable.

"Thanks, did I hurt anybody last night?"

"Nah, the bartender had just had enough and called me. Said you wouldn't let anybody haul you up to your room, so I had em bring you here. You went right to sleep. As usual."

"Sorry, can I leave now?"

"Soon as you finish your coffee," he said with a grin.

"I appreciate it fer sure. Can you unlock the door and let me out to sit across the desk from you?"

"Come on out. I have never locked you in. You've always been able to walk out anytime you wanted. Last night no different from all the other times."

Morgan nodded looking a bit sheepish and took a seat to look at the constable.

"Coffee's good."

The constable nodded and then took on a steady look into Morgan's eyes.

"Not my place to give advice on how a person should live Morgan. Lord only knows I got plenty of my own downfalls. But..."

"Go ahead. I been sleepin' in your cell and I'm drinkin' your coffee. Guess ya got a right to speak your piece."

"Alright. Well, it's like this. I know about your wife and figure that's what takes you to the saloon most nights."

Morgan started to object to bringing up Ellen, but the constable held up a hand.

"Let me finish. That's why I take it easy on you. I lost my wife ten years ago. Not trying to say I know how you feel but I know what I went through and I didn't handle it any better than you are. I did some checking on you and I know you've been a fairly good man. Scout, Texas Ranger, soldier, even a stint as a sheriff in some small town a bit west of here. I think it's about time you get to moving on. You're still a young man. Why don't you think about making something of the rest of your life instead of supporting the whiskey industry practically by yourself?"

It took until spring, but he made his way to Independence and the MTO bunch where he again took out a wagon train. During that long haul he decided that he would head back west and find a piece of ground to settle onto. He bought a wagon and supplies and agreed to take the small group to Oregon without charge.

His plan wasn't firm, but he thought that at least he could build a place and spend a year grooming it. Then, he would see. Maybe he would stay. Maybe he would move on. He really didn't know. He really didn't care. He only knew that Ellen would not want him living like he was living.

He knew he would never take out another wagon train. Let someone else risk what he would now have to live with for the rest of his life. He would return to Independence, get the names and addresses of the next of kin of the dead and write them all letters explaining what had happened. Of course, they would all blame him, as he believed they should. Especially since he had survived when the rest had perished. To the family of the Brackett woman and the child, he would also explain that he had hopes that they might still be alive and that he planned on trying to find and rescue them.

When he got back to Independence, he went to the building that had held the office of the Missouri To Oregon Transport Company. Their sign was gone! A bakery had moved in. He went inside and was overwhelmed with the smell of fresh baked bread. He bought a loaf of sourdough and asked what happened to the former occupants. The baker said that he heard they just moved out without notice. He said one day they were in full operation and the next morning everything was gone. The landlord had rented the space to him a month or so later.

When the transport company disappeared, all their records did too. Bert Morgan had no way of notifying the families of the ill-fated wagon train. That had been his only reason for coming back to Independence. He was the only one who knew what had happened, save for the military on the coast, from which no communication would be forth coming. With no communication to the contrary, the families would assume that their loved ones were safely setting up housekeeping and clearing land as planned.

His heart was sick that he couldn't contact them. He spent a couple days trying to track down the company's whereabouts but ran into dead ends at each attempt. The town constable was as surprised as the landlords that the three men who had run the operation had just taken off without a word. More upset were the folks who had paid their deposits and been left holding the bag. Several had handed over money for the purchase of schooners that the company had assured delivery at a better price. The constable figured they had absconded with several thousand dollars of other people's money. Complaints had been filed, warrants issued and wanted posters were already printed. There was a $150.00 reward being offered for the arrest of the three and recovery of the money. Of course, no one really thought the money would be entirely returned but any amount would be better than none. Morgan knew little of the men's backgrounds. They had been established freighters, evidently, before opening the wagon train business. A freighter Bert had known from the war years had told him they were looking for men who knew the west. They would pay good money for knowledgeable wagon masters. Bert had been sheriff of a town some fifty miles south and after a disagreement with the mayor, took his leave of the place with a nasty taste in his mouth. He was considering his options when the opportunity presented itself. He had talked with Palsey Bingham mostly. Bingham had been the main man, the general manager, he called himself. He was a big, robust fellow with a sideways grin and loud voice. German Manweiller and Guffey Louden were his two partners. He hadn't taken a liking to any of them, but they had paid him half up front and the rest when he returned. His two previous trips had worked the same way. On the last of the trips, he had decided to make his home in Oregon. For that reason, he was willing to guide the small group of wagons for no wages. He did have his own wagon though, his oxen driven by Jake Conley, the son of Brett and Sarah Conley. He paid Jake the going rate and had no complaints about his work. Jake had died along with the rest.

Bert Morgan was no bounty hunter, but he decided to go after the fugitives anyway. He didn't care about the money, but he cared a lot about those records. He felt a driving need to tell the families what had happened. After talking with a half dozen folks that had gotten to know the outfit over the past five years and adding what he had known of them, he was sure they would be headed for Santa Fe. They had often talked of the opportunities of shipping from Santa Fe to parts of Mexico.

For the first time in a long time, Bert Morgan had purpose. He was driven.

It took weeks to arrive in Santa Fe. He still had the spunky roan that he had been given by the Dragoon lieutenant. The big horse was not what the black had been, but he was close. He just didn't have quite the stamina so travel for long distance was some slower. The dusty little village seemed to be teaming with life. Whites and Mexicans intermingled without much regard for one another. Freight wagons were lined up along the street near the livery stable. After looking closer, Bert noticed a second livery a block or so down the street. If anybody was going to know about the runaway teamsters, it would be these operators.

Walking into the nearest livery and letting his eyes adjust to the dark, cool barn, he could hear an argument toward the rear. Two men were in a heated debate over a wagon.

"Look Arch Walker, I paid good money for that junk. You said it was sound. Had I been able to look it over afore I put down my cash money, I would have told you where to go."

"And I'm tellin' ya'll that it was plum good when your youngin' took it outta here. He musta drove it over them rocks out your way to break down them tires like that. That ain't my fault and I ain't given you a pence back fer it. And that's that!"

The first man slammed his hat into his leg and stormed out, nearly running into Bert on his mumbling way.

Walker threw down a pitchfork he'd been holding and for the first time noticed Bert.

"Oh, didn't see ya there, what do You want? I ain't got no wagons until next week."

Bert couldn't help but smile a bit.

"Not lookin' for a wagon. Just a bit of information."

"Oh. Well, whaddaya wanna know?"

"I'm tryin' to find some old friends of mine. I heard they might be hereabouts. Names of Bingham, Manweiller and Louden, ya know of 'em?"

"Yeah, I knowd of 'em." He spat a string of tobacco juice at a mouse that was sneaking up to a grain sack. "If they be friends of yourn then I got no use for ya'll cuz I got no use for them all."

Bert grinned and took a step forward sticking out his hand. "Well, I might have overstated that friend deal. Bert Morgan is my name. They skipped outta Independence, Missouri with a bunch of money that didn't belong to 'em and I'm lookin' to git it back."

Walker's expression soften just a bit and he reluctantly shook hands.

"Sounds to me," said Bert, "that they ain't done much to improve their ways. How do you know of 'em?"

"Ah, the scoundrels happened in here a month or so ago with three double sets uh wagons and trailin' several head uh nags. Said they were settin' up shop for haulin' goods to Mexico City. Well, they paid for my services for two weeks in advance, so I naturally took 'em in. Well sir, they didn't have no luck gittin' no loads so after about ten days, they came in and took their leave. Wasn't till the two days later that I went to put some paper money in my big cash box that I found it gone. That box had every spare dime I put away during the last three years. Except for this place here, it was everything I had. We ain't got but a constable here and he won't leave town morn about three feet to git a thief. Ain't no other law around. I don't dare leave fer fear uh that low down Draper down the way taken over my business. I think they were headed fer Mexico but ain't got no way uh knowin' fer shore. Ya trackin' the scum?"

"I am. How long ya reckon they been gone?"

"Uh, nye on tuh a week I spose. Whuchya gonna do when ya find their sorry hides?"

Bert ignored the question. "How much ya reckon they got from ya?"

"Nearly three hundred dollars, blast their spineless soles. Any chance ya might git some of it back to me if ya git the drop on 'em?"

"If I git the drop on 'em, I'll bring back what money I can. I'm after papers they might have from Independence more than anything else. I been in the saddle for two weeks now, I sure could like a bath and a shave and a night in a bed. Any decent place hereabouts?"

"Yeah, Annie C's Way Stop just over there. Has rooms to rent upstairs and her café downstairs. Keeps a clean place and has good food, too. The Golden Shoe has good whiskey, right next door, if'n ya be a drinkin' man. I don't partake much myself, but I might have just one with you if'n you was tuh buy?" He looked hopeful.

Bert Morgan left the roan with Walker, took his saddle bags and walked slowly across the street. Annie C., it turned out, was a beautiful bit of a woman with amber-colored hair and full lips that broadened into a warm smile when Bert walked through the door.

"Good afternoon. Have a seat. Coffee?"

"Yes Ma'am! That would be right nice."

Bert studied her as she picked up the pie plate, fork and coffee cup from the next table. She was maybe thirty but not much more, he thought. The few lines in her face did nothing to distract from her beauty. Her long hair reached halfway down her back in a French braid. Her figure was something to behold. The kind that made a man wish he was married and settled down and had a woman like her to come home to. He noted no band on her left hand but there was an indentation where one had been. A groove like that would take years to make. He was surprised at himself. Not since he lost Ellen had he given so much as a second glance at another woman.

She took the dishes through a door in the back and when she came back, walked directly to him with a cup of steaming coffee and a tiny pitcher of milk for him to mix in.

"Are you hungry? Supper won't be until six thirty, but I've got some chicken soup and fresh made bread if you're interested."

"Yes Ma'am, both would be right nice."

When she brought back the food, she smiled that smile again. Morgan wished she would not do that, it was mesmerizing. He smiled back and thought, "You keep smiling like that, I might just fall in love before I finish my meal." Of course, he kept that to himself.

"Haven't seen you here before, new in town?"

Bert was just ready to take his first bite of the slice of hot bread and butter. He put it back on the plate instead. If he was lucky enough to have conversation with such a creature as this, he wasn't about to do it with a mouth full.

"Yes Ma'am, I mean, I'm really just passin' through. But Mr. Walker over yonder suggested I might be able to git me a bath and bed hereabouts. This here eats is bonus to my way a thinkin'."

Annie smiled and sat down in the opposite chair. Bert's heart jumped.

"Well, where are you headed Mr. ...? I don't believe I got your name, Mr. ...?"

Bert leapt from his chair. "Oh, excuse me Ma'am, its Morgan, Bert Morgan."

Her smile became a laugh, the most wonderful laugh Bert Morgan had ever heard.

"Please, Mr. Morgan, do sit down. And please, call me Annie. And yes."

"Ma'am?"

"Yes, I have a room for you and a bath. Supper is in about two hours. It's included in the price of your room. The bath is fifty cents and the room is two dollars. The tub is out back in a lean-to. Takes me about half an hour to heat enough water so give me some warning."

"Well, as I'm afraid you can tell," Bert admitted with a slight blush, "I been on the trail fer a while so I would like to git that there bath as soon as it works out fer ya."

"Well then, you enjoy your bread and soup and I'll get on with heating it up."

Then she was up and gone and out the door to the back. He savored the soup and bread. She came back in before he finished eating and refilled his cup. She cleared off the dishes and then once more took the air out of the room with her smile. This time she brought a quarter of an apple pie and held it out in front of him. With a shocked look he started to reach for it. She pulled it back and her smile turned impish.

"Tell you what, you get your bath out of the way and I will buy this piece of pie for you. I want to hear about where you are going and where you came from. I don't get many folks to talk with this time of day. Finish your coffee and by that time your bath will be ready."

"Well Ma'am, uh, I mean Annie, you got yourself a deal. For that pie, I'll tell you way more than you will care to hear."

They both laughed. He leaned back in his chair and sipped his coffee while listening to her tinker in the kitchen behind the door. He had just swallowed the last drop when she called out to him.

"Come on back here, your bath is ready."

Dutifully, he followed her directions and went through the back door to the lean-to. It was closed in by the back wall of the café and on two sides. A curtain hung open at the front, suspended on a wooden rod across the top. She stood beside the curtain with a towel and washcloth folded over her arms.

"Soap's on the stand beside the tub," she smiled. "Soo Yung has a laundry just down the street. You want him to wash your clothes while you wash? Might not be dry in time?"

He took the towel and washcloth.

"I got a clean change in my saddlebags."

"Where are your saddlebags?"

"Oh, I guess I left em on the chair where I was asittin.'"

"Well, you toss those dirty duds out here on this sawhorse and I'll get your saddlebags. I'll take your dirty things to Soo Yung. He will charge fifty cents to do them, is that alright?"

"I'd be much obliged Ma'am, uh, Annie."

He lounged in the tub until the water started to cool and was wishing it still had more warmth.

"Cover yourself, I'm bringing in hot water."

He made a desperate attempt to pull the washrag over what he needed to cover just in time as the curtain was pushed open and she came through with a big bucket of steaming water. He knew he was blushing, and this made her laugh. She slowly poured the water over his feet.

With a chuckle as she poured, she said, "Oh, don't be so silly, I have three brothers and have been married twice. Besides that, I do most of the doctoring in this town. There isn't anything about a man I haven't seen before."

"Well, with respect Ma'am, I ain't been one of them that you seen and I don't wanna be if it's all the same."

He tried to speak in somewhat of a convincing voice but couldn't contain his laugh. She laughed too as she left, pulling the curtain behind her.

Feeling good after shaving and taking a bath, Morgan went back across the street to the livery. He wanted to make sure his horse would be taken care of properly. He was pleasantly surprised to find that not only would his dollar buy two nights lodging for the animal but grooming, too. He pulled the saddle off, put the roan in the stall that Walker pointed to, and used a coffee can to pour some grain into a trough.

"Well Walker, I'd be happy to purchase us a drink, if you care to accompany me to the establishment across the way."

He tried to sound uppity, but it didn't sound at all natural and he didn't know enough vocabulary to make it work. Walker jerked his head up as if having won the biggest hand of poker ever won. The grin was ear to ear.

"Well now, by jingles, I believe I have just enough time for that drink and as many more as your bank account warrants!"

He was already leading the way to the saloon, "Course, you understand, I don't partake of the spirits much myself but, for you I'm gonna make an exception." His strides were long and fast. "I'm just doing this cuz I knowd you don't have any friends hereabouts and I'm sure nuff the hospitable type, I am." He was pushing through the batwing doors.

Morgan had barely made the middle of the street. He glanced to the window of the hotel/café in hopes of catching a glimpse of Annie. She was standing in the window grinning at him. Her look and slight shake of her flawless face told him that he was just one of many to be hooked into buying drinks for the man he was trying to catch up with. He shrugged and grinned back at her.

He was early for supper. She was visiting with a local man and wife when he walked in. She looked up and smiled widely. "Come on over here Bert." He walked to the table. "Mr. Morgan, this is Constable Zebediah Bicksteader and his lovely bride of thirty-five years. Thirty-five years as of today! Mrs. Bicksteader helped me get my start here in Santa Fe."

The constable stood up with a welcoming smile to shake hands as Bert removed his hat. "Zeb will work just fine."

"Well, now, congratulations! That there is some sort of accomplishment, it surely is. I'm honored to make your acquaintance on such a special occasion." He was proud that he had gotten out what he considered a pretty fine speech.

As Constable Bicksteader sat back down, "Thank you, nice to meet you, yep I feel purdy good about myself. Not every man could hold on to a woman such as mine. She is more than any man could ever hope for."

His wife blushed appreciatively and patted his hand, and looked up at Bert and Annie, "I've just kept him fooled all this time. I tell him every day how lucky he is and he just keeps believing me. Won't you join us Mr. Morgan?"

Bert, his hat still in his hands, said, "Gosh, I sure appreciate your askin' Ma'am, but I sure wouldn't feel good about keepin' you two lovebirds from a private anniversary supper." He smiled and finished with, "But Ma'am ifn' he gits outta line you just give me a holler, I'll be right over there."

All four laughed. He shook hands with the constable, bowed slightly to Mrs. Bicksteader, then took a seat at the same table as earlier. Annie sat down across from him.

"What with your bath and all, I didn't get to find out what you're up to."

"Well, it's a long story but maybe I can give you a short version."

He shared his mission but had a hard time trying to explain why he felt so strongly about notifying the families. To his amazement, Annie put it into words that exactly fit what he was feeling. He had a hard time thinking about leaving to chase after the scoundrels. This woman was captivating in a way that he had never experienced. The little smile lines at the edge of her eyes, coupled with the twinkle when she found something amusing, stuck solid in his heart. He would definitely be back.

It had been a long haul for Morgan since leaving Santa Fe. Weeks of following the roughly hewn roads and trails south through New Mexico Territory and eventually to the banks of the Rio Grande at the newly established settlement known as Rancho de San José de la Concordia. It was the founder,

Hugh Stephenson and his beautiful bride of local aristocracy that made his two-day rest both comfortable and informative. Señor Stephenson knew of the Missouri to Oregon conmen. They had wanted to establish a transport business in his village, but the American frontiersman's acute sense of human nature quickly recognized their unscrupulous character and bid them leave. They at first rebelled but Hugh Stevenson had not accomplished all he was known for by being easily dissuaded. The low-life stature of the trio soon led them to understand that not a request, but rather, an order, had been issued. They were gone with the morning light. With the heavy wagons, it had taken Bingham, Manweiller and Louden much longer to make the trip from Santa Fe. They had cleared out of Rancho de San José de la Concordia just two days before.

The señor and señora had spent more than two hours over a wonderful supper and wine with Morgan. They were gracious and told him that they were sure that the men he sought would be crossing into Mexico at the ferry a day's ride down the river. As he sat his horse the next morning and took hold of the mule's lead-rope, Hugh Stevenson came across the dusty little street to bid him farewell, good hunting and an invitation to stop again on his way back to Santa Fe.

With the mule in tow, Morgan touched the flanks of the roan and clicked his tongue, urging the reluctant animal onto the plank boards of the ferry. Still, the roan hesitated. Morgan dismounted and led the horse onto the boat. The mule walked on without interest or concern.

The stocky, good looking Mexican introduced himself as Julio Mendes. His shiny black hair curled around his ears and above his thick eyebrows of the same color. His eyes danced and he displayed perfect white teeth when he smiled. He said he had left his village, two hundred kilometers to the south when he was just a boy. He made his way into Texas and lived with his aunt who insisted he attend school. In his early twenties he worked on a cattle ranch then did some prospecting without success. Then one day he saw some wagons trying to cross the Rio Grande. Two of the three swamped and lost most of their belongings. Two of the oxen couldn't get loose and drowned. From that experience he got the idea of a ferry business. It took him a month to find this area where the water flowed quietly but was still deep enough to accommodate the barge, even with a full load. Over the years his reputation for safe crossings grew. Folks came several miles along its edge to pay to cross.

Bert had paid his fare before getting on but when he reached the Mexican side and had led the animals off, he dropped the reins and walked back to the skipper. He handed Julio a quarter more. It was small pay for the information he had gained from the man. Julio grinned and held up the quarter.

"Hey, this gives me an idea. Perhaps I should ad *information* to things I charge for."

Morgan laughed and said, "Maybe so. Could be a dangerous business though."

He now knew exactly where his prey lingered. Julio Mendes had told him that they were arguing about where to go next as he hauled them across. The largest man had said they would camp down the river a bit and rest up for a couple days since they were now safely in Mexico. A rider coming upriver to the ferry had mentioned that three men were camped in a grove of trees near the cliffs. Julio knew the area well and described it in detail to Morgan.

Julio agreed to keep an eye on his mule until he returned. Maybe a couple hours, maybe the next day. He hobbled the mule in a grassy spot just down the river a hundred feet from the ferry and unloaded the animal's heavy burden. From one of the packs he took out a Mexican cross-belt of ammunition and put it over his head and across his chest. He checked the rifle and his pistols. Mounting the roan, he took to a sustainable gate down river, toward the MTO bunch.

It was coming on dusk when he reached the spot told him by the ferry man. He tied off the roan and worked his way up onto the cliff overlooking the camp. He was close enough to hear their voices but could not make out the words. The sun had now lowered below the horizon. He took off his hat and slowly, silently eased his way to a point where he could look down on them. He exposed the top half of his head for only a moment, but his trained eyes took in everything in an instant. He knew where every bedroll laid, where the fire was, where the men were sitting against their saddles, where their rifles rested, and that just Bingham had a sidearm strapped on. The other two-gun belts hung on broken branches ten feet away. It was obvious that they felt safe on this side of the river. No American lawmen would come after them in Mexico. They apparently never gave a thought to bounty hunters.

Morgan wiggled back away from the overhang, retrieved his hat and rode a way farther down the river, out of sight of the banditos. He hobbled the roan and using his lariat, made a makeshift corral with three sides of rope and the river for the fourth. It was a small area for the horse but there was a bit of grass to munch on and water to drink. He took off the bridle and saddle and laying them outside the corral, settled down for a nap.

When he woke up it was full on dark and the stars were dancing in the sky overhead.

The moon was nearly full and bright in the east. He guessed it to be near midnight. He stood up and stretched. The horse was standing quietly in the center of the roped in area with one hind foot raised up on its toe. If he wasn't asleep, he was at least content. Morgan strapped on his gun belt and the bandolier. He took off his spurs and laid them beside his hat next to the saddle. Taking the rifle from its scabbard he started the eighth mile walk back to the Bingham campsite. When he reached the overlook, he quietly took a look over. The campfire had turned to coals with a slight glow. The three MTO thieves lie sound asleep. Bingham snoring noisily. Bert withdrew and walked back upriver to where he could easily descend to its level. He moved easily along its moistened bank making not a sound in the sand.

It was without a hitch that he roamed through the camp gathering up the rifles and pistols. The only one he didn't get was Bingham's who still had his strapped to his side. He carried the weapons fifty yards away and stashed them under some brush. He was

just starting back when he heard the shout!
It was Manweiller. Clearly visible in the
moon light. Morgan moved into the shadow
of the cliff and watched and listened as
Manweiller was yelling about his guns come
missing. Now it was Louden making the
same harried announcement. Morgan
couldn't help grinning even though it was
going to be a different set of circumstances
now. Bingham was up and had his pistol in
his hand, crouching in a shooting position,
looking all around. He could hear
Manweiller.

"I'm tellin' yuh; my rifle were right there
and so wust my pistol!"

Louden started yelling before
Manweiller finished his admonition.

"Don't be telling me that I took your
durn guns! Mine are gone too you fool."

"Shut UP!" It was Bingham. "Shut up
and listen! Whoever stole my rifle may still
be around. Keep your eyes open and listen."

Morgan didn't let a muscle flinch. His
breathing was slow and steady. Years of
being in tight and dangerous situations had
taught him to be patient. He needed to figure

out how to get that pistol out of Bingham's hand. He pulled his rifle into position and took aim at Bingham's gun hand. He needed the man to make a half turn to his right. If he shot the gun out of his hand with him looking directly in Morgan's direction, the bullet would go right on into his gut. Morgan had killed enough men in his time. Three while acting as a sheriff ten years back. Six as a Texas Ranger. How many while fighting wars and Indian raids would be only a guess. Way too many. He didn't want another on his conscience. His position was the only way in or out of the camp unless swimming was an option. The overhang of cliff curved around and into the river behind the MTO bunch. This fact now played against what Morgan wanted. It kept Bingham's eyes glued right his way. He decided to take a chance and threw a rock high up onto the overhang just above Bingham's head. The reaction was immediate. With blinding speed, Bingham whirled and sent two rounds into the exact place where the rock had first hit. The man was fast and accurate! Just as quickly he turned back to face Morgan and two more rounds came whirring past his head. Bingham must have heard the whisper of his clothes as he threw the rock. It just took a blink of an eye for the sound to register on Bingham's psyche. He reacted to the louder and closer rock sound first and then to the launching point. Morgan knew what revolver Bingham was using. It was the same gun Morgan had strapped around his waist. He knew, too, that it held five bullets and now only one remained in Bingham's .36 caliber Paterson Colt. Now, as he leveled the rifle at Bingham's kneecap, he hesitated. Bingham was walking directly toward him with Manweiller and Louden following single file behind him. Another five feet and Bingham would certainly see him. There was no cover, just the shadow that kept him hidden from a distance. Bingham still wasn't sure someone was in the shadows. This was evidenced by his reaching into his gun belt for more cartridges. Suddenly, Bingham stopped and flipped open the cylinder and began to eject the used casings. Manweiller chose that time to say something to him and Bingham turned to his right to look back. Morgan's rifle barked and Bingham's hand was ripped in two. The gun went flying as he screamed in shock, grabbed his hand where his thumb and two fingers were now missing. He rolled on the ground, moaning between repeated curses. Manweiller made a grab for the pistol but found that the one unused bullet had fallen free and disappeared in the dust. He also cursed, but out of fear and frustration.

"You blew my hand off you son-of-bull-spit! Why'd you do that to a poor man like me?" Bingham was sobbing now.

Louden had grabbed a couple shells from Bingham's belt and snatched the Colt from Manweiller. He was shaking badly and having a hard time getting the thing loaded.

"Don't you do that Louden! I'll shoot you in the belly if'n you try it. Don't do it!" Morgan warned.

Louden was shaking and mumbling unintelligibly while Manweiller simply sat on the ground, hands on his knees and head hanging dejectedly, Bingham curled up in a ball by his feet. Then Louden pointed the gun at Morgan's shadowed place and fired two quick shots followed by several clicks as the hammer fell on empty chambers.

"OK Louden, you've had your fun. Toss that thing out in front of you as far as your puny little arms will do it."

Louden cussed again and threw the gun fifteen feet in front of him.

"Who in tarnation ARE you?" It was Manweiller.

"You got any more guns or knives hidden away?" Morgan moved into the moonlight.

"Bert Morgan?" Louden was indignant. "What are doing here and why are you shooting us?"

"Yeah, it's me alrighty. About those other guns and knives. Got any more of em'?"

"NO! The knives were on our belts and you tookem' all, blast you!"

"Alright then, you best get somethin' tuh wrap around Bingham's hand afore he bleeds tuh death. I'll just keep this rifle pointed right at ya whilst you do that. Manweiller, you just sit right where you are. Nice and cozy with your boss man."

"He ain't my boss no more. We're even-steven partners now. You still ain't told us why you hunted us down. We ain't done nothin' to you."

Louden returned with a dirty set of Bingham's long johns and tore off a sleeve. Bingham groaned as Louden wrapped his bloody stub in it.

"You best git a stick and use the other sleeve to make a tourniquet up a ways on his arm to slow down the bleedin'. Grab hold of a piece of fire kinlin' to turn it tight."

Louden did as he was told. "Now, you gonna tell us what you're doin' here? Reckon you came to rob us, but I sure didn't think you were the type."

"Well, you're partly right. I am gonna take your money. You see, there's a powerful big bunch uh folks you hurt bad by takin' the money they trusted you with. I aim to give it back to 'em. All that you stole and whatever you didn't. The other thing I want is all the records you kept about that last train I took out. Where you got those?"

"You came all this way and shot us for records?" The words from Bingham were disbelieving. They were issued forth with grunts.

"Yup, that's it. Now, where are they?"

Manweiller spoke up, "We give you the money and the records, then what? What happens to us? You let us go?"

"Yup, that's how it works. You get all that for me, Manweiller?"

It was during this exchange that Bingham fainted away. He toppled onto Manweiller's feet. Manweiller pulled one foot free and shoved the big man away. He stood up beside Louden.

"We'll go get it out of the wagons."

Morgan chuckled and said, "Uh, I don't think that'll work boys. Louden, you raise up Bingham back up to a sittin' way and then sit with his back leaning against yours. Come on! Do it now! Manweiller, you git your lariat off your saddle and tie 'em up."

When the two men were tied up to Morgan's liking, he followed Manweiller to the biggest wagon. After half an hour of poking around in the dark they finally found the right box of records and list of folks on his wagon train. The list gave the address of someone to notify for each family. Next came the money. One big box that had over four thousand dollars in it. All of it neatly packed into money bags with notes inside saying who it came from and when and what for. Bingham might have been a lot of bad things but being a sloppy bookkeeper wasn't one of them. In a separate bag was two thousand more dollars indicating profit the outfit had made. Morgan took out three bundles of twenty dollars each and left them laying in the back of the wagon.

"What's that for?" Louden ask.

"Just want what I came for. You're gonna be needin' a sawbones for that hand uh hisn'. Even here in Mexico they charge for their services. It'll take a bit uh money to git started up in business again. You had done a good service in Missouri. Too bad you went greedy. Maybe you can do some good again. Just be doin' it down here. Wouldn't recommend you goin' back across the river no more. You left a trail of folks from all over that would love to git their mitts on you."

With that Morgan tied up Manweiller and checked once more to make sure Louden and Bingham were still secure.

"I'll be back in the morning and turn you loose. You git loose on your own I'll hunt you down. Just as well stay put."

"What about our guns and knives?"

"Well, you can sure go look for 'em tomorrow after I let you go. They'll be found at the bottom of the Rio Grande there."

Actually, that was a bit of a truth stretch. Only the knives ended up at the bottom. The guns were packed on to his mule along with the records and the money. As he left the next day, he had already led the horses and mules of the bunch back to the ferry where he tied them off. He untied only Bingham knowing it would take the one-handed man longer to untie the others. By the time Bingham, Manweiller and Louden had made their way to the ferry to retrieve their mounts, Morgan was across the river and well on his way back to Santa Fe.

Annie C. was surprised to look into the dining room and see him sitting at the table.

Surprise, relief and then just a touch of giddiness. She smoothed the front of her dress and primped her hair before coming on through the door. His back was to her but there was not a doubt who she was looking at. He hadn't seen her yet and when she came around in front of him, he jumped to his feet and quickly took off his hat.

"Well, well," she smiled, "You finely got hungry enough to come back."

He chuckled as she motioned for him to sit back down. "I'll be right back to join you," She said as she went to another table to pour some coffee.

She came back with a steaming cup and set it in front of him.

"OK then, first things first. What can I get for you to eat?"

"I know it's almost noon but if you had any of those breakfast biscuits you make, I sure could go for a few of them. Maybe some of that sausage gravy if you have any left."

"Well, this is your lucky day. I sure do have some of both. I'll get the gravy heating up, but the biscuits will probably be cold."

Neil James

He nodded his approval. She went into the kitchen and came right back out with coffee of her own.

"Well that didn't take long," he said.

"No sir, been a change or two since you were last here. I hired me a cook. Mariah. She's good too. Gives me a chance to catch up on things and talk with wayward travelers that happen to show up wanting breakfast at noon."

There was that big wide grin that he had been thinking about regularly since the day he left weeks ago.

"Now, tell me all about what you've been up to. Don't leave anything out."

He was looking deep into her spellbinding eyes and for a moment couldn't think what to say.

She felt his gaze and reached over to pat his hand. "Come on now, give."

He cleared his throat and told her as much as he could about the past few weeks. He said that he had just got back into Santa Fe and had gone straight to the constable's office to turn in the money but Constable Bicksteader wasn't there and the door was

178

locked. "I took the money over to Walker's, but he wasn't there either. I stashed it in back of one of the stalls. Any idea where Zebadiah might be?"

The smile had left Annie's pretty face and she shook her head slowly.

"Ten days ago, Albert Winston came into town and robbed the general store. I think he musta been drunk. He came out of the store with what little money Frank had in his cash box, he had just opened and so he just had a little change in the box, anyway, Albert stumbled down the stairs into the street and Frank came out behind him yelling that he was a no good scoundrel. Zeb just happened to be making his morning rounds and Frank yelled at him about what Albert was up to. Zeb stepped off the boardwalk just across the street from Albert and told Albert to drop the money and his gun. Albert told Zeb to go to hades and just up and shot Zeb square in the heart. Doc said he was probably dead before he hit the ground."

"Sorry to hear that. How is Mrs. Bicksteader getting by?"

"The story gets worse. Somebody went to their house and told her what had happened. She came running down the street screaming for Zeb and when she got there, she threw herself down on him and, Bert, she had a heart attack and died right there on top of him."

She had tears in her eyes.

"What about Albert whatever his name is? Did he get away?"

"Oh yeah, nobody wanted to chase him down. He's a good shot with a rifle although men folk here say the pistol shot that killed Zeb was just pure luck. They don't think he intended on hitting Zeb at all. He just stood there after Zeb fell. Just looked in shock at what he'd done. He's just a kid really. Maybe seventeen or eighteen. Never has had a lick of sense. After a bit he turned all around in a circle brandishing that gun and yelling that he would kill anybody that chased after him. They said he looked like a scared jackrabbit."

"So, who's stepped up as the constable?"

"Well, nobody really. Several of the men that live here in town get together at night and walk around just keeping an eye on things. They all have good jobs or run businesses of their own, they don't want the job. A good many of the men have started wearing guns just in case."

They sat and talked until the biscuits and gravy came out. They were on a huge platter and beside them was a thick steak.

"Figured you might be hungrier than just the biscuits."

She stood up then and walked over to a table with three town women. She sat down with them for a couple minutes and then went to bring them tea.

Straight up six o'clock, Morgan came down the stairs from his room and sat down for supper. The tables had been moved together in a single row to accommodate a family style of serving. Already there were hot rolls that filled the room with aromas that made him drunk with hunger.

Other people were at the table. A man and woman that appeared to be traveling. A preacher with a white collar under a black coat. Two men that looked as if they had just rolled into town aboard a train of dust and dirt. He nodded at the group and took off his hat as he sat down. He listened to the light, casual conversation as he ate. The atmosphere was congenial, and he enjoyed it.

He finished his meal and was looking to Annie for another cup of coffee. The traveling couple had left the table for their room and the riders had ask about the chances of getting a bath. Annie had sent them down the street to Soo Yung's place. She told them that she didn't have baths available after 3 o'clock but Soo Yung was accommodating any time of day or night and would also do laundry if they wished. The preacher still sat at the table reading his bible and sipping the last of his coffee. Two men walked in and said hello to Annie. They took off their hats and ask for coffee.

"Mind if we join you Mr. Morgan?"

It was the taller and older of the two. He spoke with a nervous smile that quivered a handlebar mustache. Morgan had seen him at the general store before he left to chase the MTO bunch. He had told Morgan that he had owned the store for quite a long time. Inherited from some relative. Morgan couldn't remember what all he said but he felt alright about the man. The other fellow didn't look familiar. He was a short, heavily built man of fifty, dressed in a city suit with a watch chain sneaking from within his vest, looping around and disappearing into a watch pocket. He nodded but did not smile or speak.

Morgan looked at each man and shrugged, indicating the chairs across from him with his coffee cup.

Annie finished pouring the coffee and the three men all nodded their appreciation. She offered a refill to the preacher, but he declined, excused himself and left the table.

"Mr. Morgan, you might not remember me, but I run the Mercantile here in town. Name's Sam Rucker. This here is our mortician.

"Howard Demery," said the mortician. Still no smile but he did hand him a piece of paper with his advertisement on it.

Bert Morgan took a quick look at it and set it aside. "How can I help you gentlemen?"

Rucker cleared his throat and started in, "Well, sir, we were just kinda wondering how long you might be staying with us here in Santa Fe?"

"Have I worn out my welcome already?"

"Oh no, certainly not! Well, we just thought you might be thinking about settling here in our fine town. You see, I'm the Mayor and Demery here is the chairman of the city council. Well, you see we were just wondering if you might be looking at settling down here."

"Oh for cryin' out loud Sam!" Other than his name, the first words out of Demery, "We want you to be our town constable. How about it?"

Morgan was about to take another sip of coffee but stopped halfway to his mouth. Without taking his eyes off the chubby undertaker, he slowly set the cup back on the table.

"Come again?"

Rucker started to say something, but Demery cut him off, "We heard how you took care of those desperadoes down in Mexico. We think you could be just the man we need. Ever had any law work before?"

VENGEANCE ON THE MOUNTAIN

Morgan looked over at Annie who had been listening from near the kitchen door. She raised her eyebrows and just shrugged. He looked first to Demery and then to Rucker and then back to Demery.

"A little but I'm headed back to Missouri to send out letters to some folks."

"Fifty a month plus a house to live in and your necessaries for the job." Demery didn't mince words.

It was Rucker's turn, "We got us a post office and mail leaves outta here every Tuesday and Friday on the stage. Might take a little longer from here than from Missouri but if you wrote and mailed those letters from here, I'll just bet they would get where they're going before you could get back to Missouri, write them and then mail them from there. How about it?"

He had a point about the letters. He did have all the names and addresses.

"You got a bank here?"

"No sir. Not today. But Colonel Randolph has joined up with some investors and they're opening one just next week!"

They looked confused and a bit befuddled.

"How about it Morgan? You in or not?"

Morgan had to keep back a smile. This undertaker took no prisoners.

"Tell you what. Let me take a stroll around the town and think on it for tonight and I'll let you know in the morning."

Demery nodded and briskly stood up jabbing out a podgy, short fingered hand. Rucker looked up and taking the cue also rose. The three shook hands, the pair tipped their hats to Annie and left. The room was suddenly quiet and empty except for the two of them.

"Guess I'll be the one paying for their coffee," he said as he watched them go and noted that they hadn't left any money.

"Well, that was interesting. Hope you don't mind my eavesdropping. Seems like folks hereabouts forget that I have ears. Oh, and don't you worry about the coffee. They both have a tab with me. They'll pay, including a tip," she smiled.

Morgan nodded with a chuckle, "What time you close up? Interested in taking a walk and telling me about the town?"

"I'll have Mariah keep an eye on things for the next half hour. She's already got things pretty well picked up in back and most likely won't be more than somebody wanting coffee or a piece of pie. Everybody knows I close at seven on weekdays."

She went into the back to tell Mariah what they were up to. On her way to the door she snatched a white shawl from the coat rack.

They walked and talked as Morgan took in the little town and Annie pointed out things of interest. It was a good town. They passed other couples out enjoying an after-supper stroll in the cooling air. They all nodded and said hello. It was an easy atmosphere. Morgan liked what he saw. He liked walking with Annie!

The next day he had agreed to take the job for a month or until they found themselves a new constable. His decision seemed to suit Annie. Before telling Rucker and Demery he talked it over with her. She made only one recommendation.

"This town started collecting taxes from day one. It's got money and they can pay more than fifty dollars. How about getting them to foot the bill here at my hotel until they get the house back in order?"

The house was owned by the town and Constable and Mrs. Bicksteader had lived in it. The city had a little basic furniture for it but that had been put in Arch Walker's livery loft because the Bicksteaders had their own. It would be at least a couple more months before their daughter and her husband were scheduled to arrive from Iowa to sort things out.

He had followed her advice and they had quickly agreed but added the stipulation that they be allowed to negotiate with him after a month should he decide he was still thinking of leaving. In six months, an election was scheduled to elect the first Sheriff for the area. He would be based right there in Santa Fe. They thought he might be interested in running for that position.

The first three days had been spent going through everything in Constable Bicksteader's desk and arranging things to his liking. He felt little pangs of guilt when he changed things that Bicksteader had obviously thought through and placed as he felt best. Fortunately, for the most part, he agreed with how Bicksteader had left the office.

He had moved the money into his room but would sure be glad when that bank was opened. No one, excepting Annie, yet knew that he had retrieved the money. Word had it that he got back the records he went after but not the money. It was one of those rumors that just caught fire and each day the forest of hearsay just fueled the flames. It was an inferno that he saw no need to squelch until the money was safely in the bank. Nobody but Walker, the stableman, had lost anything in Santa Fe so it was of no real interest to the locals. Once the money was safely in the bank, Morgan would send notice to the law in Independence and they could arrange to come get it or have it transported.

The shot could be heard echoing through town in the dark of the night. Most of the town was asleep. It was just the timing that made it work out the way it did. Bert Morgan was making his final turn around the town before calling it a night. A few young men were still in the saloon but outside of an occasional burst of laughter, they were just quietly drinking their beer. He had just passed the open door, looked in, waved at the bartender and continued on when the shot came. It was most certainly from down the side street ahead of him. He trotted to the turn and saw two men. One was flat on the ground, unmoving. The other was running right toward Morgan, until he saw the big lawman blocking his way. The runner immediately stopped and fired two quick shots.

"I got no quarrel with you fella, but you don't git outta my way I'm gonna shoot you for sure."

It must have been then that he saw the badge flicker in the moonlight. He raised his gun and fired twice more.

Morgan, ever calm, aimed his revolver at the man's left foot and pulled the trigger. Instantly the man cried out and dropped his gun. He was dancing around in circles on one leg, holding the injured foot in his two hands. Morgan walked up to him and kicked away the gun.

"You sit right down here son and don't think about moving or I will fer shore shoot off your other foot."

Two from the saloon came running around the corner. Morgan picked up the gun and put it in his waistband.

"One of you fellas run over and get the doctor. Hurry fast! Other one keep your eye on this one whilst I check on him down yonder."

The man who had first been shot was laying on his back. His eyes were open in apparent shock. He was dead, a bullet hole through his chest.

"Doc says to bring him over to his office. He'll meet us there," called one of the men.

Doc Ross was a young man of no more than thirty-five. At six foot two he loomed above most other men in town. He was from Hawaii and had come with his father to join an expedition to the northern mountains looking for beaver. Somehow, he had ended up in Santa Fe. Being that he seemed to know a lot about medicine, he was welcomed into the community that had no doctors. Within a short time, he had helped so many people with everything from disease to broken arms, he was able to build a small house and rent an office. That was all anyone knew about him. What happened to his father no one knew.

Morgan told one of the gathering crowd to go get the undertaker but he needn't have bothered. Demery was already headed into the side street. First time Morgan had seen him smile.

As soon as they got the kid with the shot-up foot into the light of Doc's office, one of the fellows recognized the shooter. It was Albert Winston. The kid who shot Constable Bicksteader.

One of the young men who had carried him in exclaimed, "Why, we otter just hang him right here and now!"

Bert Morgan pulled up a chair just far enough away to not interfere with the doc's activities, "Oh, I reckon not. But, how about we git him fixed up and have us a real live trial? Be a lot more entertaining and who knows, we might have us a legal hangin' after that. Think on that, a gallows and a hangman. That would be some show wouldn't it?"

As excited as he sounded to the others, it was all for show. Bert Morgan had seen men hang and he hated those memories. But, given the circumstances, he would say whatever needed to get through a fair trial.

The people had elected a judge two years earlier. They paid him for each time he traveled the fifteen miles from his village. They had decided that someone from another town that didn't know much of the folks in and right near Santa Fe would be the perfect choice. He would be more impartial. And he was. He was a Mexican of good standing, a rancher, a businessman and he was very well read. What he didn't know about the law he made up for in common sense.

The trial came two weeks later. A jury of six men was chosen along with a prosecutor and a defense attorney. Morgan had tried to get one of the Winston kid's family to come speak on his behalf, but they seemed to be glad to be rid of him and wanted nothing to do with the trial. The judge made sure the man chosen to represent the kid spent time trying to get some kind of information that might not get him hung. The kid was only mad at having his foot shot and being caught. He was defiant and without remorse. He said he was proud to be known as the gunman that killed Constable Bicksteader and felt he was justified in killing the man on the side street because he was going to turn him in.

The trial lasted less than an hour and that included time for the jury to deliberate.

When the judge asked for the verdict, the foreman stood up and cleared his throat.

"Guilty as hell, judge!"

The crowded room sent up a cheer and the kid's cussing at them could hardly be heard above the roar.

The chant of "Hangim' now!" began to grow until people out in the street began to echo it. The judge sat there and waited for things to calm down.

When the crowd quieted again, he calmly proceeded with, "Alright, Señor Albert Winston, you have been tried for the murder of two men and the jury has reached a verdict of guilty on both murders."

Once more the chant began, "Hangim' now, hangim' now, hangim' now!"

Again, sitting back in his chair behind the table, borrowed from Annie's eatery, the judge, his chaparral patch of white eyebrows, pitched disapprovingly downward toward his nose, waited. His long fingers tapped impatiently on the table, but he otherwise gave no indication that he would rush the quiet. It took a bit longer this time but gradually the chant died away and his honor was able to continue.

"Therefore, it is the decision of this court that, on the first day of this coming month, you shall be hanged by your neck until you are dead. This court is adjourned."

The cheers drowned out the last sentence and the judge stood up and walked over to the chairs where Morgan and the kid sat. The defense attorney had already raced out, headed for the saloon. The judge told Morgan to get him out of there and be quick about it. Morgan took hold of Winston's arm and with the judge right behind, quickly led them out a side door and to the jail. He did it so fast that most people didn't even realize they were gone.

People started showing up in Santa Fe ten days before the hanging. Some coming from as far away as Mexico to the south and Colorado to the north. Many more from towns and villages within a hundred miles. Each day saw more and more strangers in the little village. Annie's was full every day. Ones that couldn't get a room were offering to 'buy' rooms from those that did get lucky. Townspeople were renting out floor space for sleeping and meals while others joined with folks camping in tents. Many just slept under the stars and hoped it didn't storm.

Bert Morgan brought in two Texas Rangers from the neighboring state. Two friends he had served with several years prior. All three had their hands full as the frantic pace and anticipation grew. Drunk and disorderly was the crime of the day it seemed. Since jail space was not available, those charged were simply fined and sent to wherever they were sleeping. For some, that was just on the steps of the saloon. As soon as it opened in the morning they would go in and capture a table and stay there, drinking, cussing, laughing, and shouting. Table space was as much a premium as hotel rooms. Often disputes erupted over someone taking a place at a table only temporarily vacated while its first occupant took a needed outhouse break. There seemed to be an endless list of reasons why disturbances persisted.

The biggest came when Big Bulla Banks came in on the stage from neighboring Albuquerque. Big Bulla was nearly six feet tall, claimed to be forty, but the lines in her weathered face showed closer to sixty, even through several layers of powders and rouge.

Whether she be forty or sixty, nobody was going to argue the point with her. Well, almost nobody.

Bulla got off the stagecoach and walked directly into the saloon, directing the driver to deposit her bags in the hotel. She didn't look back or give the driver a chance to protest.

David Erikson had gone up to the bar to get a hardboiled egg, leaving the seat beside his brother momentarily unoccupied. Bulla hesitated only a second to scan the scene before strutting to the chair. Bulla's walk was more like the swagger of a proud duck. She sort of wobbled with her shoulders back, hands open to her sides with fingers parallel to the ground, separated wide, pointing away from her body, her head high, her more than ample bust leading the way and threatening to jump out of the very low cut, swishing dress, with each step. Her large, protruding derriere swung from side to side, timed perfectly with each waddle. Her silver wig was perfectly manicured.

Without invitation or asking, she plopped herself into David Erikson's chair.

Every voice went silent when Bulla walked in. Bulla was used to this and made no notice. Every man in the place sat, unmoving, watching her every move. Most had their mouths agape. Bulla gave forth with the slightest hint of a smile as she sat down. She turned to David Erikson's brother and said, "What's your name, sweet thang?"

The boy gulped and recovered enough to answer, "Hardy Erikson, Ma'am."

"Well, sonny, you win. You get to buy the first drink for Big Bulla Banks. Don't be long now. It's been a thirsty ride all the way here from Albuquerque. Hurry along now."

"Uh, shore thing Ma'am. What should I say you'd want?"

"Just tell the barkeep that it's for Bulla. He'll take care of the rest."

When his brother joined him at the bar, David Erikson ask why he didn't save his seat.

"Never occurred to me. Just look at her."

"Well, I can tell you this. That there is durn sure my chair and I plan on runnin' that old witch outta it."

"I don't know Davey, there's just something about her that tells me to go easy."

David might have done well to heed his brother's advice. Instead, he walked over to stand above Bulla. Instantly Bulla was uncomfortable with that.

"Don't stand behind me sonny. If you got something to say to me, stand on the other side of the table to say it."

"I'll stand anywhere I want lady. If'n that be what you are, which I doubt. You took my chair and I want it back. Right now!"

Bulla didn't move but did reply, "I told you, don't stand over me like yer doin."

David Erikson then made his biggest mistake. He grabbed Bulla by her wig and yanked. Her bald head was revealed but this, too, didn't seem to cause Bulla concern. Young Erikson then added to this affront by using his buttocks to try to bump her out of the chair.

"I told you I want my chair back!"

At this exact time, Hardy Erikson arrived at the table and tried to pull his brother away. David Erikson was drunk and now incensed with anger. He jerked away from his brother and in doing so, fell full force against Bulla who was just repositioning herself in the chair. She toppled to the floor with David Erikson sprawled on top of her. This, in turn, knocked over the vaquero sitting in the next chair. He jumped up and grabbed the back of Erikson's shirt, jerking him off Bulla, who took the opportunity to strike out. Bulla was heavily, sturdily built. The uppercut she threw came directly to David Erikson's gut. This was followed by a right to his jaw from the man whose chair had been knocked over. Two other men at the table leapt up to help Bulla. David's brother had picked up her wig and held it out for her. She snapped it from his hands and slapped it onto her head as David struggled to his feet. It was then that David's excess of booze came back up and he covered one of the fellows that helped Bulla stand up. That man reacted instantly by shoving David away from him.

Hardy then decided to help his brother and landed a left followed by a right to the man's face. The man's buddy took exception to this undeserved assault and retaliated with

Neil James

his own left and right that sent young Hardy to the floor directly behind Bulla. She stepped back to avoid the conflict and tripped over Hardy. She slammed into the table behind her knocking two men down that had been watching the events. They perceived that another man at Bulla's table had somehow pushed her and not knowing who it was just jumped two other bystanders and, the brouhaha quickly took over the entire saloon releasing pent up energy and anticipation. Soon, nobody knew who or why they were fighting but only that they were happy to be involved. The fight spilled out onto the street.

Bert Morgan and his two Ranger deputies were in his office going over how the hanging was to take place when twelve-year-old Orey Bilker came running in to tell them what was happening. It had only been twenty minutes since the last fight outside the saloon had been taken care of. Bert sighed, grinned and shrugged at his two helpers. They all hurried down the street and immediately realized it was out of control and would continue to be no matter what they attempted. They took up positions across the street and sat down on benches in front of Walker's Livery to watch. It didn't really matter who started this bruhaha, nobody would be going to jail or even fined. No gunshots were heard, and nobody was coming out in a bloody mess. The saloon owner had made so much money during the past few days that he wasn't going to complain much about the few broken glasses and chairs. He had, the minute the verdict was delivered, doubled his prices. As things quieted down, the three lawmen made their way to the batwing doors of the saloon to look in. Tables and chairs were scattered throughout, and the bar was lined with men laughing and slapping each other on the back. Just one table was upright and occupied. At the table sat Big Bula Banks. Cozied up on each side of her and laughing loudly at something she had just said were the Erikson brothers.

Jacob Limer was nearly eighty years old, but his short-cropped hair was still coal black. His wrinkled face was highlighted by a long, pointed nose with wide, elongated nostrils that looked as if they could house a mouse. Unlike the hair on his head, his great handlebar mustache had turned white. The ends of the mustache were colored a yellow brown resulting from decades of wayward tobacco spit. Thick eyebrows highlighted the eyes that betrayed his harsh exterior and danced as he made occasional observations of his trainees' work. His back was straight and strong, as was his character. Jacob carried broad shoulders under his long johns that represented the only upper body cover he owned. In hot weather he peeled the top down to be bare chested. If this offended onlookers, well, Jacob would never have shown any acknowledgement.

Once a month or so, when the undergarment became so soiled with dirt, sweat and grime, that the stench overcame even Jacob, he would take them someplace up the creek and wash them. No one knew if the body got washed at the same time. He didn't believe in taking a day off when work was to be had and he didn't believe in taking any advice or criticisms from anybody his junior and nearly everyone in Santa Fe was his junior.

Jacob Limer was, and nobody questioned this, the town's foremost carpenter. He had just completed his latest project. With Jacob giving orders and working harder than his two young helpers, the trio wrapped up the work. The two boys, both in their late teens, had been sent off to get their pay while Jacob stood back to critique his work. Nearly two stories high with perfectly spaced stairs. He spat at a stray cat without looking away from his creation. Hands on his hips, he walked all the way around it and finally satisfied, gave an approving nod and grunt. He had a twinge when he thought about this fine structure being dismantled in just a week's time. This, after all, was the result of not only his work but also of his design. In a way, it was a work of art. This, most anyone would have to admit, was one fine gallows!

The night before the hanging, it was not probable that even one person got more than a couple hours' of sleep. So full of people were the streets, that it was next to impossible to drift off even for a few minutes. Every person not owning a business, waited anxiously for the event to be finished and all the hordes to depart. Business owners had mixed emotions. They, too, were sick and tired of the whole circus, but they did enjoy all the extra profits.

The morning oozed with hungover boozers lying around on boardwalks and in the town square. Many, while still able to walk, had made their way to the gallows and slept beneath it so as not to miss having a good position the next day.

The sun began to drive away the morning coolness. The main streets had a thin layer of mist from the moisture caused by a welcomed but very short and light sprinkle combined with every imaginable other liquid from human and animal contributions. Above the six-inch layer of mist, shadows of buildings slowly travelled from the west to the north as the day progressed.

In Annie's, the wafting aromas of frying bacon crossed the street and danced its way into Bert Morgan's consciousness. He was about to comment to one of his friends when the door opened and Annie came in, her hands full of loaded plates. That she could carry four heavily laden platters with such grace was somehow astonishing to Bert. He jumped to his feet as did his two friends and quickly took the platters, all the time saying thank you. The young prisoner stood at the barred door for his breakfast. Bert walked Annie back to the hotel and they agreed that a buggy ride in the country would be a great idea once all got back to normal.

The proceedings were scheduled to begin at 11:45 with the trap door on the gallows to drop at precisely noon. The kid had at first been indignant, loud, boisterous, and generally a pain in the butt. For the last 48 hours, though, his mood had changed dramatically as realization began setting in. This was not a joke, and nobody thought he was tough or that he was a true bandito. He began to feel lonely. Not one of his family had come to see him. True, he had tried to kill his brother with a pitchfork, slapped his mother numerous times and told his stepfather that he would never be the man that his real father was. Never mind that his real father had abandoned them when he was just three years old and been shot dead trying to break into a widow's hacienda. Now, the reality that he was indeed going to be dead in two days came clearly into focus. Throughout the night Morgan had heard him sobbing. Morning had brought resolve to the kid, but the bravado crap was gone. He was quiet and when Morgan handed him his plate of breakfast the kid had actually said "thank you".

"OK, kid. Time to go. It's 11:45."

"Do you think it will hurt much?" The kid's voice was shallow and shaky.

"Don't know. Never been hung before. If it works right, I'm thinkin' ya won't feel a thing."

Outside, the street was empty except for the town kids that wouldn't be allowed near the gallows. They were all gathered across the street to get a look at the murderer as he was led to his death. Some of the parents had tried to keep the morbid details from their kids but of course, some older kid had told a little brother who took in every detail and quickly explained it all to a wide-eyed audience at school. Most all the girls found it disgusting and didn't want to hear more about it. Most of the boys immediately started figuring out how to watch every aspect that they could.

Bert Morgan led the cuffed killer to the bottom of the stairs. Here, they were met by a priest who whispered something to Albert Winston. The boy nodded and said something in return. Morgan put just a touch of pressure on the boy's arm to get him to take the first step up the stairs. Albert Winston jerked involuntarily as if shocked. He looked at Morgan and then tried to take a step back.

Morgan clamped down on the boy's upper arm and firmly urged him forward.

Tears were streaming down the young face and unlike the killer that he was, he looked to be a kicked puppy. Unable to see through the tears he stumbled and whimpered as Morgan kept him afoot. At the top, the judge asked if he had any final words. Albert had composed what he thought should be the kind of statement that would be uttered by a tough, belligerent gunman. Morgan had heard him rehearsing earlier in the week. Now, at this opportunity, the kid could only get out a stammering, barely audible, "Don't wanna die."

With that, the Judge descended the stairs and gave a nod to Morgan. A black hood, precisely cut and sewn by Lilith Sevy, the best-known seamstress in the area, was placed over Albert's head. It came down just past his shoulders so the rope would go over it without risk of it riding up. Morgan put the noose over the hood and pulled it tight enough so as not to come off. At this point the kid's legs began to buckle. Morgan and one of his Ranger friends each grabbed an arm to steady him.

Morgan whispered in Albert's ear, "Come on son. Be tough. Don't let them see you as a coward."

The boy straightened a bit and raised his head some. Morgan looked over to the man handling the drop lever. It was Jacob Limer. "I see it this way, I built the damn thing, I should be the one to operate it."

Morgan looked at his pocket watch and when it struck 12 noon, he nodded and Limer pulled back on the handle. The trip mechanism worked as designed. The trap door upon which the kid stood fell away with a bang and the boy followed it down. There was pop and for just a second the rope groaned its protest as the weight hit. The cross bar that supported the hangman's rope creaked eerily as the weight swung back and forth. All this was easily heard because the crowd was completely silent.

Bert Morgan and his two friends walked down the stairs followed by Jacob Limer. Walking under the gallows, Bert watched as Doc checked for any sign of life. After a moment, the doctor turned, head down, and slowly walked away without looking at

Morgan or anyone else. Albert Winston, the hardened killer, the sobbing child, was dead.

"What does the C stand for? I don't think you've ever told me."

"You're right. I never have told you." Annie chuckled and Bert looked at her with a puzzled expression.

"OK," she said. "Here you are, it stands for my last name. Cominiskia."

Bert tried to repeat it but got it wrong on two feeble attempts. "Yeah, well, I reckon I'll just stay with Annie C."

They were sitting in the shade of their favorite tree by the little stream that seemed to create a gurgling beyond the babbling of most such brooks.

She laughed that enchanting laugh that made him want to swallow her up in his arms and whirl her around in the sagebrush flavored air. He knew he had fallen in love with her but had no way of knowing if she felt more than friendship for him. Many times, he had thought the setting was right to tell her how he felt and each time he cowered. What if she didn't feel the same? It might ruin their whole relationship.

He was thinking of just that when with playfulness in her eyes, she spoke. She reached over and took his big hand in hers. Then she smiled.

"When are you just going to say it out loud?"

"Say what out loud?"

"When are you just going to say out loud what you say with your eyes every time we are alone? When are you going to say I love you?"

He was speechless. He had no idea he was so transparent. She squeezed his hand again. "Well?"

He tried to clear his throat, "I reckon I didn't know how without scaring ya off."

"Well, you're not going to scare me off, so?"

"How did ya know?"

She laughed again, "Men are so thick headed. Women just know these things. I've known how you felt for weeks."

He could feel himself blushing. It was not a feeling he was familiar with nor liked.

"I guess I just don't rightly know how to say what I feel sometimes."

Another squeeze on his hand. It felt good.

Let's try this. You just say what I say. "Annie C., I love you."

He grinned. "Annie C., I reckon I love you."

"Alright, now I can say this. Bert Morgan, I love you too."

The wedding was a celebration for the whole town. They hadn't planned it that way, but things just seemed to get out of hand. Annie had too many friends to decide who should and should not be invited. Bert had become highly respected for his service to the community and he had several men who wanted to stand up with him. He had chosen his best man solely for the fun of it. Old Arch Walker, the first man he met when he arrived in Santa Fe, the owner of the livery stable, the man who had suggested he go to Annie's place. It only seemed fair that Walker, the crusty old fellow that Morgan had grown to know and like, be the one beside him. Walker nearly panicked when Morgan approached him with the idea. At first, he said it was pure foolishness and not for an old fool like him. But Morgan had told him to think about it for a while and he would check back. The more Walker thought it over the more he warmed to the idea. He got to thinking about what an impression it would make on the residents of Santa Fe. After he told Morgan that he would do it he went to Sam Rucker and ordered a brand new topcoat, string tie, shirt and pants. Sam Rucker had measured him with great effort, he and Walker arguing about every detail, and finally telling Arch Walker the final damage. Walker stomped around the hardwood floor cussing about the outrageous price. Sam Rucker was successful for many reasons, not the least of which was his ability to close a sale.

"Alright you old son-of-a-buck, you've talked me into making a concession. I can't afford to do it you understand but, since it's for Morgan and Annie, I'll throw in a new set of long johns and stockings."

That stopped Walker in his tracks. "By durn, ya do that and ya got yersef a deal!"

"Don't ya tell nobody what ya talked me into doin' for ya. Can't have the whole town beatin' me down like you just did. I need half up front."

The half up front was more than his total cost of everything. The other half would be his profit. He couldn't contain a smile, but he hid it from Walker. It came to only a very small portion of the three hundred and twenty-eight dollars savings that had been stolen from Walker by the MTO bunch and that he never expected to see again. He had stood, for once, speechless when Morgan had handed it to him. The night before the wedding, Walker spent more than an hour cleaning and polishing his best pair of old boots.

PART THREE

1858

Santa Fe did eventually find a new Constable but only after Bert Morgan agreed to a position with the U.S. Marshal Service. Annie presented the couple with two children and his pride in them was obvious any time someone mentioned them. Both were strong from the beginning. The first born was named Randall Garrett Morgan. When Rand, as he became known, was in his second year, he was joined with a little sister named after his mother and maternal grandmother.

Annie Wixon Morgan, known as Sis for her entire life by all that knew her, would pull her father around like a puppy tugging on a stick. Bert Morgan had a reputation for being tough as iron but those who knew him could see that when it came to his family, he melted like hot molasses. Annie ran the household and her business and was unchallenged by Bert and the two kids. Sis controlled the tough man's heart to her every whim. Annie constantly told Bert it was shameless. But she said it through a smile.

Through all those years and all that happened since the wagon train raid, Bert Morgan never forgot about the woman and the baby that somehow disappeared. He thought about them often and had told Annie everything he could remember. The two of them had talked about what might have happened to them. On two occasions he had gone into Idaho territory on Marshal business and had taken the opportunity to scout the miles around the area of the raid. He was unable to make any sense of what may have happened. As the years passed, he found himself more and more disturbed. He had made sure every family knew what had happened that night. Some of the families had banded together to upgrade the little cemetery created by the dragoons. To only two families could he give no finality. The families of Bernie and Martha Jean Brackett.

He had early on determined that it was the Warm Springs Indians that had been the raiders and assumed they had taken the woman and child. He had taken a *tamed* Warm Springs scout with him to translate and help retrieve the two ten years before. This trip had nearly cost him his life, but he had survived and learned to his satisfaction that the raiders had not in fact taken the captives. He was told that the band had killed everyone they found right there on the spot. What then had happened to Mrs. Brackett and her son?

His frustration was something he thought he might forever live with until just a month earlier. He had taken into custody a highwayman wanted for murder and robbery. While in Bert's cell the man babbled on and on about anything and everything. Bert paid little attention until one sentence jumped out like a rifle shot.

"Yep, some of them trappers swear that white woman and her kid really like livin' up

there in them Owyhee Mountains with them injuns."

Bert was sure this was the Bracketts. He took a hiatus from his duties as a Marshal to make one more trip. This time was different from the others. He was optimistic about his chances. Also, this time his son, Rand, who considered himself a man, accompanied his father.

Annie was always concerned when Bert was away but she had somehow found a way to immerse herself in running the Way Stop so as to not constantly have a knot in her stomach. This time was completely different. Her son would be with Bert on a trip that would likely take upwards of six weeks, maybe more. Rationally she knew Bert would die before letting anything happen to their son, but it was the irrational that spooked her.

She had gone with Bert on one of the trips some five years earlier and she knew how rugged the country was. She also knew that he was convinced that the Brackett woman and her baby had been scooped up by Indians.

Annie also knew that her son, though very young, was very mature and levelheaded. Bert had taught his wife and two children to shoot very early on. He had gathered an arsenal of confiscated firearms over the years. Annie carried a hidden, two-shot derringer with her all the time, but she was very good with a rifle or small revolver as well. Sis was proficient with the same size revolver and with the long gun her father had given her.

It was Rand that felt a driving need to become expert with a sidearm. Rand, who idolized his father knew the kind of work and the dangers involved that kept Bert away so often. By the time he was ten, he felt that he needed to be the man of the house when his father was away. Showing unusual maturity, he had convinced Bert and Annie to let him practice. Now, he was indeed an expert with a handgun.

Still, Annie was worried. More about the plan of finding the Indian tribe than anything else. Word had it that this mountain tribe was peaceable unless others first caused trouble. That was all conjecture.

Nobody Bert talked with had any actual contact with them.

It was a trip of a thousand miles each way. Through towering mountains and endless deserts. All the way, Rand more than carried his weight and never complained. He asked about certain geological sites and tried to make mental notes as they went. Without being told, he periodically stopped to look back over the trail they had just covered.

"You think somebody might be following us?" asked Bert on one of those stops.

"No sir, just want to know what to look for on our way back. Remember? When we was out hunting one time, you told me a trail has two views, one coming and one going back. I'm just trying to figure the look both ways."

"Smart, keep at it."

Although there was really no need, Bert wanted Rand to see where all this began. They spent the night there and before dark, Bert pointed out the direction and some landmarks that they would go toward the next day. They had skirted those mountains on the way to the river. Now they would tackle them head on.

Rand awoke to the harsh bray of the mule that carried much of their goods. Bert was already up with the fire ablaze and coffee boiling. Rand sat up on his blanket and vigorously rubbed his lengthy mop of brown hair. He brushed it out of his still sleepy eyes and reached for his boots. He had been at war with the new boots for the entire trip. They were hard to get on and harder still to get off. They were still stiff, and the heels were higher than his old ones. He had to admit though, they stayed in the stirrups better and that had been a blessing when coming down steep slopes. With a grunt, a stomp and another pull, the second boot gave up and took its place on his foot.

"Coffee smells good."

"Well, I was about to pour it out if'n you hadn't finally crawled out. It's comin' on noon."

Rand laughed, "Somebody forgot to move the sun, then."

They ate leftover bacon and biscuits made the night before. It was still early when they rode away from the old wagon pieces that stood as memorials to that fateful night so many years before.

"How far you figure we got to go to reach the village?"

"Wish I knew. Shoot, I don't even rightly know there is a village. Just got to try."

They rode on for two hours and only now and then caught sight of the Snake River far below. By the time the sun had climbed to its highest point, they were well into the mountains with nothing but mountains to be seen in every direction. They stopped to eat some jerky and more biscuits and rest the horses. They had come across a copse by a small lick of water. It was obvious this had been the stopping place for a lot of travelers over the years. Bert was quite sure none had been white.

"Pa, there's a lot of flint or obsidian workings here abouts."

He held up a cupped handful of splinters and broken arrowheads.

"That's good eyes. I'd say we're headed the right way, these fire fixin's over here are perty new. I'd say the last month or so. Ain't seen no rain."

"Looks to be a well-traveled trail headed out over there, Pa."

"Take a closer look and see if there be any hoof prints."

Rand followed the trail a way and returned.

"Lots of prints. Some not all that old. None are shod."

Sunset, and the pair had settled down around a fire, a pot of beans cooking. Supper would be a while. Rand was busy stirring up some hardtack. The biscuits wouldn't be like his mother made at home because they had no eggs or other ingredients. Just flour, water and salt. They would be more like a cracker than a biscuit. Still, they would taste just fine given the circumstances. The amount he was stirring up would cook on the coals and make good snacks along the trail between meals. He couldn't understand how his father could seemingly go forever without eating while Rand was always hungry. The hardtack was a lifesaver for him. He finished working the dough into three ten inch by ten inch squares of a half inch thick and laid them on the coals. He would need to turn them over in a few minutes.

As darkness engulfed the campsite and the firelight dimmed to just the flickering of coals, three young warriors watched from a hundred yards away. They had seen white men before, well, one of the three was himself white, although none of them thought of that. Their interest was in what the man, and a boy near their own age, were doing here. Were they hunting? They didn't look like hunters somehow. Trappers? No traps were evident. It was puzzling. They would report back to Buha in the morning. Tonight, they would settle down nearby and keep watch.

At dawn, Rand finished loading the pots onto the mule as the sun broke over the horizon. Bert tightened the cinch on his horse and swung into the saddle.

"I'll take the mule for a bit."

Rand handed him the lead-rope and mounted up. Bert led the way up the trail that Rand had checked the night before. It was an ancient trail that had been used for hundreds of years. Since last night Bert had the chills up his spine. He could feel that they were being watched. Who was there he couldn't say but it was Indians for sure. He was confident that no white men were up in these hills.

He hesitated to tell Rand. Why make the kid nervous for just a feeling? Then he saw the flash of movement. In the rocks two hundred yards forward, above and to their left. It was just a flash, but he hadn't survived all these years by missing things like that. It was no longer just a feeling and it was time to let his son know.

They had been talking off and on since leaving the camp. Talking now, if he kept his voice under control, shouldn't alarm those watching.

He started with a laugh that he hoped would further dispel any hints of his knowing someone was out there.

"Hey Rand, gotta tell ya something."

"Another one of your silly jokes?" he chuckled.

"More like a challenge. See if you can handle it. When I taught you to play poker, after ya learned the basics, what was the next thing I told ya to practice?"

"How to keep a straight face no matter what I had in my hand? Is that it?"

"That's it. Now, I'm gonna tell you something and let's see if you can keep an absolute straight face. No changing how you sit the horse and no looking around no matter what. Think you can do that?"

"Well, sure. But Pa, this don't sound so much like a game."

"It ain't no game. Remember, don't change a thing."

"I'm ready, what's up?"

"Don't look around. We're bein' watched. Have been since last night."

"Ok, I'm keeping the poker face but why didn't you tell me. Where are they?"

Bert's horse stumbled on a loose rock and Morgan pulled up on the reins. The horse regained its footing and continued.

"I just had a feeling about it last night and right up till just now when I caught a glimpse."

"So, what'll we do Pa?"

"Not a thing. You can look around like we always do but don't look hard to our left, up in the rocks. That's where I saw something."

Rand did as he was told. He looked around like he had been doing the whole trip and even pointed out an unusual rock outcropping off to his right. They rode on, following the trail. The three young braves finally rode off to get ahead of them and let their head man know of the intruders. Bow Shooter, Knife Thrower and Clay Brackett got back to the summer camp of their village and went directly to Buha. They told of what they had seen and estimated that if they continued at the current pace, the white men would arrive at the knoll overlooking the encampment within about three hours. Buha decided to take the three boys and Coyote Killer with him to meet these two men before they were close to the camp. Other warriors wanted to go but Buha didn't want to make the visitors feel in danger more than necessary.

Bert and Rand made the corner in a deep wash and came face to face with five

Indians sitting their horses. As they reined up, Morgan immediately noticed two things. First, one of the teenage boys was white. The other thing he noticed was that the boy was riding an aging horse that brought back memories. The horse was a big black, the one he had ridden for two years before the wagon train raid. He brought his attention back to the two adult warriors.

"We're here in peace."

He was shocked when the bigger of the two answered in fully understandable English.

"You are in Shoshoni mountains. No white mans here."

Bert and Rand both looked at the white kid.

"He is my son. His mother my wife. No other white man."

"I was the wagon master on the wagon train that brought you the boy and his mother," he gave a quick nod at the black horse, "and my horse."

"Not our raid, Warm Springs. I find boy and mother after."

"I have made many trips trying to find the boy and his mother. I need to tell their family what has become of them. Can I see the mother?"

"You camp here, I ask mother if she want see you. You not go more. I come back morning. You go no more."

With that they spun their horses and were gone. Simply turned their horses and rode away.

"Pa, you think they will try to kill us?"

"I don't think so. I think they would've already done it if that be what they were thinkin'."

He looked around to assess the area for a possible camping site. It offered little. Still, he wanted to make sure the big Indian knew he was trying to live up to his instructions. It was Rand that spotted a small, V shaped space between two of the massive boulders that occupied so much of these mountains. Mammoth amounts of granite that appeared to have fallen from the sky or tossed there by some gigantic creature. They led the mule to the space and as Rand began building a fire, Bert took the horses back down the trail from where they had come. He filled their canteens, their coffee pot and the other pot that they used for cooking. They used deadfall of mountain mahogany to build up a good fire. No use worrying about being spotted now. Tonight, high in the mountains, the nights having gotten colder, they would sleep warm.

Bert was finding himself almost giddy. He hadn't realized just how much he needed to finish this long task. Tomorrow, one way or another he would be able to put it to rest. He tossed and turned all night. He'd drift off but then awaken, hoping it was morning, only to find barely half an hour had passed. He was up long before dawn and the coffee pot was boiling heartily when Rand rolled out with the graying sky in the east. They hadn't talked all that much the night before, both consumed with their own thoughts. This morning, Bert told Rand every detail he could think of. About the years before his wagon train days, about the raid itself but in more detail than ever before, about recuperating at the coast with the dragoons and about hunting down the MTO fellows to retrieve the records.

"As a matter of fact," he smiled and motioned toward the sidearm Rand carried, "that there gun you're carrying belonged to one of them no-goods. Fact be known, he probably stole it from some poor dandy. Too nice a rig for that fool to have paid for outta his purse."

"Uh, ya think this old rig has blood on it, Pa?"

"Naw, that fella wasn't much of a shot. Too much of a coward to have taken a chance of shootin' at somebody and havin' them to shoot back at him."

They both laughed and continued talking for more than an hour. That's when he heard her voice.

"Mr. Morgan? Are you here?"

He jumped up, "Yes Ma'am! We're over here behind the rocks, we're comin right out."

When he and Rand walked into her view, she stood with two Indian braves and her son. The group stood looking at each other for what seemed a long time, none knowing just what to say. Bert took one step forward.

"Mrs. Brackett. You haven't changed much since last I saw you."

He looked at the boy, "Now can't say so about the youngin', looks as though he grew some."

Martha Jean Brackett smiled, "Well, Mr. Morgan, you may show a year or two of wear but not much."

She pointed to the big Indian beside her, "This is my husband Mr. Morgan, this is Buha, chief of the Mountain Shoshoni tribe. Of course, this is Clay, my first-born son. This other gentleman is Coyote Killer." She continued but turned to her husband and son, "Mr. Morgan, as you know, was the leader of our wagon train. He was highly respected by all who knew him. I believe he is a good man." Turning back to Bert and Rand, "It's good to see you but why are you here Mr. Morgan?"

"Well Ma'am, I was left for dead but wasn't quite ready to quit just yet. I recovered and made my way back to Missouri. I eventually got my hands on the records of our wagon train and notified all the families of the folks that were killed in the raid. They got to move on with their lives. All ceptin' yourn. I told them about Mr. Brackett but couldn't ever tell them what happened to you and the child. It's been eatin' on me all this time. I was responsible for all of you and I couldn't protect you when the time came. I came back to the low country a few times but never could figure how to find you or what happened to you. Not till a while back when I heard about a white woman and teenage white boy livin' with some Shoshonis way up here in the mountains. That's why my son here, this is Rand, and me, decided to give it a try."

"Have you been in touch with my family? Are they all alive and well?"

"I haven't heard from them in over ten year. At that time, it was just your mother and sister. Never knowd about any others."

"My father died before we left. It was just my mother and Lilly and me."

"I have all the letters they wrote to me in that there pack on the mule. There is one that's not been opened cuz it was meant just for you if I ever found you."

Buha broke in.

"You come to our camp. You leave guns and knives here."

Morgan heard Rand start to object but put his hand up to silence him.

"I reckon we don't much like the idea of leaving our guns and knives. I give you my word we won't be usin' them as long as you and yours don't mean us harm."

Martha Jean whispered something to Buha and Buha nodded.

"Follow us but stay back just a bit," she said.

Buha, Martha Jean and Clay led out while Coyote Killer hung back to follow Bert and Rand.

"Just relax son. I think we will be fine but keep your gun hand free and easy just in case. Whatever you do, don't go makin' any uncalled-for moves."

They rode on for a couple more hours, without stopping and when they topped the knoll overlooking the village, Rand drew rein. He looked at his father, obviously nervous about continuing into the heart of what could be a hostile environment. Morgan just nodded and continued.

When they arrived, young children crowded around, looking at them with wonder. Braves stood, weapons in hand, and women continued doing chores but taking numerous glances. Three or four old men sat near a fire bed watching as Buha led the way to his tepee. He shooed away the children as he dismounted and motioned for Bert and Rand to get down. Immediately, Bow Shooter and Knife thrower began to lead the mule and horses away.

"Hold up there now!" He looked at Buha, "I wanna git them letters off that mule."

Buha said something to the boys in Shoshoni and they stopped. Morgan walked over and opened a side pack and took out a leather binder with the letters. He motioned for the boys to go ahead and returned to the tepee. He handed the packet to Martha Jean who went into the tepee and returned with two woven blankets that she placed on the ground for Buha and Morgan to sit on. She looked at Morgan and told him she would go inside and read the letters while he talked with Buha. Clay and Rand stood until Buha motioned for them to sit on the dirt. Two young women, not yet fully grown, came with a white man's metal bucket full of water and a wooden drinking gourd of some sort. The bucket was dented but didn't appear to leak. Buha took a drink from the gourd and handed it back as the young woman holding the bucket passed from person to person. Both Rand and Clay sat next to their fathers and glanced at each other for mere seconds. Their attention waiting for cues from their fathers.

"Do you think you will take away my son and his mother?"

"That's not why I am here. Not unless they want to leave. Just lookin' around here, I would guess that would take a go ahead from you. Like I said, we came here to find out what become of 'em. I owe that to their family."

Instantly, Clay jumped to his feet, "This is my family. This is where I stay!"

As soon as Clay rose, so did Rand. The move was clear. *'You want trouble, I'm right here.'* Morgan reached up to Rand's arm and gave a tug to sit back down. Buha couldn't help but break an almost imperceptible smile as he, too, tapped Clay on the side of his leg. Both boys sat back down but glared at each other.

"You may talk with my woman later. You will stay with us tonight and leave when the sun rises. Your horses are tied near the water. There is grass. You can camp there. I'll walk there with you so all will know you are a guest. You won't be bothered."

He stood up as did the others and led the way.

"When can I talk to Mrs. Brackett?"

"We will come to you later."

"Today?"

"Later."

They settled down for the wait and set up a makeshift camp. It was early but they laid out their fire and started some coffee. Together they unpacked and repacked the mule to redistribute the load and take inventory of what supplies they had left for the trip home.

"We'll keep the pack on the mule and the horses saddled."

"Do ya think we'll be needing a fast way outta town, Pa?"

Morgan smiled.

"Don't think so but no use in not being ready. Just loosen them cinches a bit."

"How long you 'spect we might wait for Mrs. Brackett to show up?"

Bert chuckled, "One thing I've learnt from other Indians I've run across, they ain't never in a hurry to consider what a white man might want, ain't supposin' these be no different. They'll be along in their own good time."

With that, Bert took to a grassy spot on his back, pulling his hat over his eyes to keep the sun out.

"Might just as well take us a little nap."

"You go ahead on Pa, I'll keep an eye on the horses."

It was late afternoon when Rand saw Martha Jean walking toward them.

"Pa, Mrs. Brackett's on her way."

Bert pushed back his hat and with some stiffness stood up. He took off his hat as she approached. He noted that except for her still blonde hair that hung long on her back, she looked more like an Indian squaw than a white woman. Her skin was tanned to a bronze that was as dark as many of the other women in the village.

"Please sit back down Mr. Morgan. I need to talk with you."

She told in detail how she had escaped the massacre and how the raiders turned out to be eastern Warm Springs and not the Shoshonis with whom she lived. She explained how Buha had rescued her and the baby. How her and Clay had been taken in by the whole tribe and cared for through sickness and pain. How Buha's sister had become as her own. How Buha had raised Clay as his own. And finally, how she had after two years, fallen deeply in love with Buha and they had married and had children of their own.

"Would you be allowed to leave if you wanted?"

"Yes, I've never considered myself a captive." She chuckled, "After all, where would I have run off to. I had no idea where we were, but I knew we would never survive without these people."

"Now that I'm here, I need to know for sure, would you want to go back home? If you do, I'll do my darndest to make it happen."

She smiled a somewhat sad, reflective smile, "No Mr. Morgan, I would sure like to see my mother and sister again, but I just wouldn't fit in anymore. These people, everything I know and love, are right here. No, I am where I belong and where I want to be. I hope you can understand."

"Don't rightly know if I understand but ain't my business to judge. I respect whatever your wishes might be. What about the boy?"

"Well, that's what I want to talk with you about. The letter, the unopened one. My mother and sister wrote that they have put aside enough money to pay for Clay's keep and education should we ever decide he needed it. My family is...was, quite wealthy by some standards. They said the money will be there whether they are or not. Buha and I need to discuss this further, but we are inclined to take that offer. Do you think he would be able to fit in?"

"I reckon that would be up to him Ma'am. He talks as good or better English as I do from what I heard. Sounds like you taught him well. Whataya say Rand? You know a lot more than me about kids nowadays."

Rand was caught off guard.

"Well, I guess he could do right well if he wanted to. Does he know his numbers and such?"

"Yes, and he knows how to read and write as well. I wanted to make sure he knew all of that just in case he should need it someday. Guess I never thought it would really happen. Mr. Morgan, if it is decided, would you be willing to take him back with you?"

Morgan looked at his son, "Whataya think son, yer sure nuff half of this two-man outfit?"

"Can I think about it for a while, sir?"

Martha Jean spoke up, "By all means, Buha and Clay and I need to do a lot of talking before any decision is made. Rand, if it comes to that, would you be willing to talk with Clay about what he might expect? It's been a long time since I was in that part of the world."

Rand looked at his father who just shrugged, "Up to you, son. Can't see no harm in it."

"Yes, Ma'am, I would do that if you think it would help out."

Clay had no interest in leaving his family and his tribe. But his father could see great benefit in having a member of the tribe be educated in the ways of the white man and who better to go than his white son? Clay's mother worried greatly but agreed with her husband. Clay spent much of the next day with Rand. They talked about what white man's school was like. They talked about what Rand had heard about colleges, only a few of which would be available to common folks. Clay gave a tour of the camp and surrounding area and told of his lifestyle. Bow Shooter and Knife Thrower spent time with them as well although they hadn't learned much English and couldn't really contribute much. Clay would translate when needed. They got permission from Bert and Buha to shoot Rand's revolver. A gun the other boys had never seen. They all took turns running a load of cartridges through it. They were surprisingly good for their first attempts. The recoil was a shock on the first couple shots, but they quickly overcame that obstacle. By the end of the day it was obvious the four boys liked each other. In the meantime, the three adults had been having their own conversation.

It was decided that Bert would keep Clay at his home for a year or so to see how far along he was in his studies and then, when appropriate, make sure he got into a college as close by as possible. Bert Morgan stayed two more days before the party of three rode out. The entire village followed them a short way up the trail, shouting good wishes and goodbyes.

Clay was quiet and reflective. It wasn't until the third day out that he began to become a bit more talkative as he began taking in new country that he had never seen before. Bert had packed three extra rifles on the mule and it had worked out well. He had given one to Buha, one to Coyote Killer and the other to Clay. Although he didn't ride a saddle, he and the other boys had fashioned a buckskin sling that held the weapon comfortably behind his back. When it became cumbersome, he just moved it to one hand or the other for long periods of time. It was the custom of warriors to carry weapons in such a manner.

They were crossing through the Great Basin when they heard the first shot. It was in the distance. It was followed by a barrage of shots. Then they saw what the fuss was about. A herd of prong horn antelope were at full run, headed directly for them. The shooting had stopped. It took only moments for the fastest four legged animals in America to outdistance the shooters range.

"We'll be needin' some camp meat, let's see if we can knock one down."

Bert pointed out a big buck near the front.

"Just shoot at that one, we don't need to be killin' more than one."

They all three shot nearly at once. The buck tumbled. The others veered off and disappeared over the horizon. Clay jumped off his horse and pulled out his knife. He was excited to show off his skills at dressing out the kill. He gutted the animal and then reached in and pulled out the heart.

"You know it is the way of some Indians to take a bite from the heart of the animal you've killed in order to show that you honor it and its sacrifice. So, who shot it?" His grin covered his face side to side.

Both Bert and Rand enthusiastically said in unison, "You did!"

Clay pulled the heart to his mouth and then stopped. Then he lowered it back into the cavity of the animal.

The grin still broad and in place, "I said it is the way of *some* Indians. Just not my tribe. I prefer my meat cooked."

They were laughing and skinning when Bert caught movement a short way off. He wiped his hands and stood up. Five men were walking their horses toward them. When they were twenty feet off, they stopped and surveyed the man and two boys. Rand had slowly moved behind the mule and strapped on his revolver. He came back around to stand by his father who had taken down his rifle as soon as he caught site of the approaching visitors. Clay had his rifle laying just two feet from where he still squatted. He had shifted in such a manner as to have easy access if needed.

The riders looked to be hardened hunters. The apparent leader had long straggly hair down to his shoulders. His skin was leathery with a two-inch scar running horizontal away from his right eye. All five wore filthy woolen pants with high leather boots. Two of them had buffalo hide coats on even though it was a warm day. The others had similar tied on the back of their beat up saddles. All had their rifles laying across their saddles with their hands on the triggers.

All this Bert Morgan recognized while they had been fifty feet away.

"Name's Hartwell. Looks like you done us a favor of cleanin' out our kill. We'll go ahead and handle it from here. You can just move on out."

Bert looked to each man separately, so they knew he was studying them. "I reckon not. I believe we shot this one after you couldn't get it done."

"Well, that could be, but the fact remains that there be five of us'n and just you and two chillins'. I guess we'll just be takin it."

"I reckon you could sure try. Rand, you take the first one to move. Don't go light on him. Shoot him right square in the middle. Clay, you and I are going to take out Mr. Hartwell here."

"Got it Pa. That's sure nuff what I'll do."

Hartwell gave forth with a laugh, but it had a nervous edge to it. "Why, you're plum crazy. Ain't no way you can git all five of us."

"You know, I reckon you be right. But I can tell you one thing. You and at least two others are going to die before we do. Just comes down to how much you want this one scrawny antelope. Now, time to make a move. You can move back from which ya came, or you can try to get them long guns into play. Your choice."

Hartwell spat out a stream of tobacco, "Well, I guess it ain't worth killin ya'll fer it. We'll just move on."

He started to rein away and then suddenly grabbed up his rifle. Before he got it three inches off the saddle, Rand had drawn and shot it out of his hands. The other four had also been caught off guard and when they whirled back around, Clay and Bert were pointing rifles dead at them.

"Whoa, whoa!" Hartwell was holding onto his hand that had blood running down the wrist. "I made a mistake. Don't do no more. We're riding out."

Bert gave a wave of his hand and said, "Well, do it now and don't be comin' back around where we can see ya cuz there won't be no stoppin' next time."

Hartwell looked down at his rifle. The action had been blown apart. He spat at it and whirled his horse around. He loped away with the other four close behind.

Nothing was said until they were out of sight.

"That was some piece of shooting son."

"I'm surprised I hit him. I was shaking."

"Well, you sure got it done," said Clay.

Bert looked at Clay, "How in the world did ya git that rifle up so fast?"

"I was leaning that way little by little and hoping they wouldn't notice."

"Well, I got to hand it to ya boys, ain't no men twice your age I'd rather have backin' my play."

The two boys looked at each other and grinned with pride.

It turned out that Clay didn't feel as out of place as he thought he might. He made friends easily and found that most of the few that he trusted with his whole story thought it intriguing that he had been raised by Indians. They were full of questions and he enjoyed   dispelling   many   of   the predetermined ideas held about Indian life. Because he was white, most people didn't have any idea that he had grown up among Indians. Those friends who did know pretty much kept it to themselves. They also realized over time that all Indians are not alike. Clay had explained that his Indian father was not bloodthirsty and didn't kill for pleasure but would go to war if attacked. Clay had kept his Indian clothes with him, and Annie had gotten them cleaned by Soo Yung and they were neatly folded and stored away. At first, Clay had objected to wearing the white man's clothes. They seemed heavy and confining. The worst part was the shoes. It took a month to get used to wearing the heavy, noisy things.

Eventually he settled in and things started to feel normal. By the time he started school that fall, he was more or less comfortable. The schoolhouse had three rooms divided as to grades.

The high school teacher was shocked at how advanced Clay was. She had been warned by Annie that he had no previous formal schooling and they didn't know where he would fit. She had told the teacher; Miss Marks that Clay was extremely bright and eager to learn. But she had no idea that he would upon arriving, be able to pass with flying colors, nearly all of the senior level tests. His mother had done a wonderful job of teaching. He spent that year and the next learning higher math, technical aspects of English and the only subject upon which he had little knowledge, world history. He and Rand graduated high school at the same time. Although Bert and Annie had supported him for much of the first year, the money from his estate had finally been processed and moved into the Santa Fe Bank. It had both Bert's name and Clay's until he turned eighteen. Clay had no issues about that. The concept of money was still something he struggled with. He could not understand why gold and silver were so highly valued or how pieces of paper could be worth anything at all. He could count it and figure how much of it he had, he understood that he could trade it for goods, he just couldn't grasp why it held value. He was

Neil James

more than happy to let Bert and Annie handle it for him.

Upon their return to Santa Fe, Bert had written a long letter to Clay's grandmother and aunt. Included in the envelope was an equally long letter given him by Martha Jean Brackett. After several weeks he got a letter back from a lawyer. He was handling the estate of the mother and daughter. Both, he said, were deceased, leaving Martha Jean and Clay the sole heirs to the estate. It wasn't huge but would be plenty to give him a head start on a new life. In addition, was the educational fund that had been set up for Clay's schooling. Enough to get him into and through college.

Clay and Rand left Santa Fe for Baldwin City, Kansas and Baker University some seven hundred miles to the northeast. The Methodist university seemed the best bet for the two boys.

Each of the two previous summers, Clay and Rand had traveled back to the Shoshoni to see Clay's family. This summer, the trip would be too far. It would more than likely be upon his graduation that Clay would next see his mother.

The first year went well for both boys. They were smart and anxious to learn. They were experiencing a world neither had dreamed existed. They spent hours in the countryside shooting their revolvers and rifles. A friend had a double barrel shotgun and they took turns practicing with that big gun. Rand taught Clay the art of quick draw and shooting from the hip. An art that was rarely heard about and almost never seen.

They earned money putting on impromptu exhibitions. Nobody in Kansas had ever seen that kind of shooting and were willing to pay to watch. Clay and Rand were all too willing to take their money as it paid for more ammunition. They were keeping up on politics, too. Although it meant little to them personally, they read with great interest about the War Between the States that had recently started. They were both adamantly against slavery as a matter of principle and Abraham Lincoln was their hero. They were learning the bible in much deeper ways than ever before. They were both especially interested in the writings of ancient scholars and philosophers like Aristotle, Socrates and Plato. They were thrilled by Shakespeare and Dickens and Jane Austen. But always, they longed for home. For their families.

Bert and Annie traveled to Baldwin City that first summer between the boy's freshman and sophomore years. They spent two weeks sightseeing and catching up before making the long journey home. The following summer the boys made it back to Santa Fe but not the next. In the last two years, they had both studied law. Finally, in the late spring of their final year, they packed up, said farewell to friends and made their way to Santa Fe.

The two boys were greeted heartily by everyone that had known them. Bert and Annie could not have been prouder. It was a small pool of folks in Santa Fe that had college educations. While both Rand and Clay were appreciative of all the attention, it soon began to grow worrisome. Clay was getting itchy feet. He was anxious to make his way back to Idaho. Back to his own family.

PART FOUR
1865

Rand said, "You should be letting me go with you."

Clay nodded, "It would be good to ride with you and show you more of my home country. But I have no idea when I might be coming back to Santa Fe and it doesn't make sense for you to ride back all that way alone."

The four of them, Clay, Rand, Bert and Annie were all standing out in front of the Morgans' house. Clay gave Annie a hug, shook hands with Bert and Rand and mounted up. Bert had urged him to take a pack mule for the long trip back to the Owyhee Mountains, but Clay had declined.

"I got more than I need right here in my saddlebags and bedroll. Don't forget, before I was a college man, I was a Shoshoni Indian. I plan to be again. But they will laugh at me just for carrying all this baggage along with me. Can't imagine what they would say if they saw me dragging along a mule."

"Don't forget to check your back-trail," said Bert.

Clay thought he saw the big man fight back a tear. He nodded to Bert, reached down and gently wiped a tear drop from Annie's cheek, took one last quick look at Rand, turned the horse to the right, and headed for Idaho Territory.

It was the first time Clay had ever been on his own. He was young but he had a combination of learning stuffed into his 21 years that few other men could claim at any age. For the first time in many years, he felt at home out in the untamed wilderness. This was where he belonged. Away from so many people. Away from a world of folks that chattered endlessly about meaningless topics that held little or no interest for an Indian. He knew the white man's world and could live in it undetected. His education could probably make him a rich man. Maybe, from time to time, he might return to that world if it would be beneficial to his family or tribe.

He pulled rein and stepped down from the three-year-old Andalusian grey. He surveyed the land around him in a slow 360-degree rotation. He walked to the edge of a nearby gulch and stood thinking about the long ride ahead. He was just two days out from Santa Fe. More and more, minute by minute, mile by mile, he felt his youth coming back. He had been and was once again, an Indian. He stripped off his wool shirt revealing his light skin that had been years without much sun light. By the time he reached his people high in the mountains of Idaho, he would be tanned as in his childhood. He walked back to the war horse and stuffed the shirt in his saddle bag.

At 15 ½ hands at the withers he easily held Clay's six-foot frame. It was the huge chest and muscled body that made the animal stand out from the rest. A gift from Bert and Annie for graduation, the Spanish Horse was one of two that they had raised and trained. The other, pure white, had been given to Rand. Bert had worked the horses for two years. Training them to live up to the breed's legendary reputation. During the month after returning to Santa Fe, Clay and Rand had spent endless hours bonding with their respective mounts. Now, Plato, the name given the horse by Clay for the animal's incredible intelligence, found great pleasure in pleasing Clay's every command. Clay had read about the breed in his studies about Mexican history. Originating in the mountainous region of Portugal and Spain when the area was invaded by the Moors. The invaders had brought their *Barb* horses. Considered the greatest of horsemen of the time, they began crossing them with the native horses of the Iberian Peninsula. After Spain regained the mountains, these crosses were further enhanced by Spanish breeders who wanted the ultimate war horse. Named for the region where they were finally developed, Andalusia, the breed has endured for hundreds of years. As the Spanish began invading the Americas, they brought their war horses and mules along. So superior in virtually every aspect of warfare, with steel and iron and horses and weapons and technique, the natives looked on them as near gods. As Spain conquered the natives the athletic Andalusian became the pride of all Mexican horse owners.

It was pure luck that Bert had stumbled onto the stud and mare on one of his ventures into Mexico. It was not something he chose to talk about because he had been forced to kill the three outlaws that had the horses. He had followed the trail of kidnappers. A teenage girl had been taken from the home of her widowed mother the week before. The woman and daughter were close friends of Annie. It was clear that no one else was capable of rescuing the girl so Bert followed their trail until he finally caught up with them. The kidnappers had met up with another man who had evidently stolen the breeding pair of Andalusians. Bert was forced into a shootout. It hadn't ended well for the bad guys. He returned with the girl unharmed and the two horses. The two colts given to the boys were the result of that breeding pair.

Neil James

Clay climbed aboard and resumed his trip. He had gone about ten miles farther and was thinking about a place to spend the night when he saw the three men coming toward him from an angle. It was obvious they intended to intersect his trail but seemed in no hurry to do so. When they were about a hundred yards off, Clay could make out the bandoleers across two of the chests.

He reached down and unhooked the leather strap that secured his revolver in its holster. Casually he did the same with his rifle. If he needed either he would be able to have them in his hands in less than two seconds.

The first man was nasty looking. Dirty black hair, hands that looked to be long unwashed. He wore what had once been an expensive derby hat. Now it was ragged and filthy. His high cheek bones seemed to hold up tiny dark eyes that were in a constant state of squint. He pulled up his nag with his two equally unappealing comrades stopping on either side of him, blocking Clay's route. None of them said a word but just sat their horses looking at him with contempt.

"Well, gentlemen, how can I be of assistance?"

The man in the middle, the apparent leader of the squalid group, looked at first one and then the other of the men beside him and then back at Clay. A wide grin developed from within a scraggly two-month growth of beard. Yellowed teeth covered with black rot in between several gaps of missing chompers revealed a high-pitched voice that didn't fit his evil appearance.

"We are not gentlemen, señor. We are very bad men. Banditos! We will now take your guns and other possibles."

Clay couldn't help himself. He laughed out loud.

"Well, yes, I can see that you are very bad men," he chuckled. "But it doesn't appear that you are much good at it. Between you, I don't think you could fill up even one of those bandoleers."

The man to the leader's right snapped back, "We got plenty to kill you!"

"That's right, we got plenty to kill you," yelled the tiny man on the left.

"What about you toothless? You think that too?" said Clay.

The leader spoke right up, "You betcha. Three of us, just only one of you."

"I don't suppose there's any way of talking you three very bad men out of this, is there?"

"We got plenty to kill you," repeated the smallest of the men.

"Alright, well try whatever it is that you need to try, I got places to go and you're in my way. Either make your move or get out of my way. Makes no difference to me."

The leader didn't seem quite as confident when he answered. "There's three of us. You can't shoot all three of us. We will kill you."

Clay had a flashback of the encounter years before with the hunters that wanted to steal the pronghorn. He smiled openly and gave a similar response as that given by Bert Morgan back then.

"One of you might get me but not before I get two of you. And, if I get lucky, I might get all three of you. You get to be first, Toothless."

He nudged Plato a step forward, looking first at Toothless and then at the other two.

"Well let's get on with it. I'm downwind of you and you stink like the skunks you are."

There was not a hint of hesitation in him and the leader just wasn't sure about this kid and the way he showed no fear. Clay didn't help the outlaw's confidence because he was still smiling like he didn't have a care in the world.

"Alright, so maybe we make mistake. We will just be on our way."

The other two were looking at him in disbelief. Neither as perceptive as Toothless. A defiant nod from their leader as he spun his nag around and started to walk it away. He was talking low to both of the others as soon as they started away. Clay watched intently and then slowly reached down and pulled out the rifle. He had it up to his shoulder with the leader in its sights when he heard him yell, "AHORA!"

In unison, all three whirled their horses around with guns raised to shoot. The rifle shot took out Toothless, rolling him off the back of his horse. With that shot Clay gave a slight nudge to Plato and the horse shot ahead and to the left. Clay switched the rifle to his left hand and pulled the revolver all in one smooth motion. A bullet screamed by his ear as he sent two shots followed by flame from the barrel of his revolver. Instantly, a scream of pain from one and a grunt from the other as the two bandits fell from their mounts.

The shortest of the three crawled, cursing Clay, toward his pistol. Clay's bullet had gone through his shoulder, but he was in shock and not yet understanding or feeling the pain. Clay sat quietly on Plato some twenty feet away. The man was almost within reach of the gun.

"Might want to rethink this. You might live if you don't try that."

The man grunted as he reached for the gun. He pulled it up and cocked it and pointed it toward Clay, "You go to hell!"

Clay shook his head, "You go first."

The bullet caught the man squarely between the eyes.

The horses had trotted off and it took Clay and Plato fifteen minutes to round them up. By the time he led them back to the bodies, three vultures were already circling two hundred feet above. Clay looked through the pockets of the men. He found no identification on any of them but did find seventeen cents in the shirt pocket of Toothless. He put the change in his own pocket. He took the bandoleers from the bodies along with the other gun belts, ammunition and guns. These he hung on the saddle horns of the horses. He knew of no settlements between him and the Owyhee Mountains to which he might take the bodies. To bury the men, he would need to use rocks as shovels. That would be the only tool available if he were so inclined. He was not so inclined. The bodies laid where they had fallen. He looked over the horses and their riggings. With some good feed and rest, all three might be worthwhile again. They had all been mistreated and half starved. Something that sickened Clay. Back on Plato, he led the string away. Looking up at the gathering vultures he gave a salute and said, "You're welcome."

These, except for the ones that took the two young tribal girls years ago, were the first men Clay Brackett had killed and it bothered him some that he felt no remorse, no guilt, no empathy. What did it say about him? He knew that Bert Morgan had killed many men, but he seemed to be saddened by having to do so. Clay was not happy about his actions but had more of a feeling of having done what needed to be done and now it was over. He would move forward and not look back. He was also somewhat surprised by his lack of emotion, or lack of fear, or whatever it was. He had felt nothing but interest when he knew he would probably have to shoot at these men. It never really crossed his mind that he might be killed. Or maybe, maybe it was more just resolve that whatever was to be, would be. He had seen that in his adopted father, Buha, many times. Perhaps that's where it came from. As he rode, he thought about Buha and his mother. He was anxious to see them again. He wondered if he would still fit in with the only family he had ever wanted. How about Knife Thrower and Bow Shooter? It had been years. Had they become great warriors? Would they now have families of their own? A few more days and he would find out.

He awakened an hour before the first signs of dawn but from the stars he knew it would come soon. The moon had moved full and bright across the night sky. No clouds obscured its illumination and he could see a hundred yards in every direction. The horses were awake and munching grass next to the spring. By the end of today he would be home. He would hold his mother in his arms and clasp wrists with Buha. He would laugh with his old childhood friends and talk of their many adventures. He would again see Eloo, his father's sister. And his younger siblings. His half-sister and half-brother. He knew they would be at their summer camp high in the Owyhee Mountains where they had spent every summer for three generations. He could almost smell the juniper wood fires and hear the creek as it bubbled past. There would be venison stew cooking by the time he got there. That would be good because he'd eaten little for the past three days.

The stars were dimmer in the east but still visible when he clicked his tongue to start Plato up the mountain ravine toward home. The big stud's ears were forward in anticipation as if knowing something special was on the horizon. The morning birds were starting to awaken with their songs and off in the distance a coyote gave one last call, sounding like two or three.

An hour went by and then another and the sun was full up and the day's heat beginning to quiet all but the crickets and their continual high-pitched chorus. The horses swatted at flies and snorted their irritation as they plodded up higher and higher. The string stopped only once, midday, to take in water at a spring. As the day reached late afternoon, Clay smiled as he topped the summit of the ridge looking down on the village. He pulled rein and studied what he saw below. The smile faded quickly.

There were no children out playing. No old men sitting around in a circle, talking. No women at the creek washing, cooking or tanning hides. He saw just one old woman, bent, with hands out for balance, inching her way across the open area between tepees. A young girl stepped out of a tepee and took her by her arm, guiding her gingerly to the opening. All the tepees seemed to be in place but it was a ghost town village. He could make out only three or four horses grazing beside the creek. There should have been dozens.

He rode cautiously into the midst of the encampment. He dismounted and let the reins drop to the ground. He walked to the tepee into which the girl and the old woman had vanished.

"Come out and see your brother Clay. I have returned to my family," he said in Shoshoni.

There was a stir of movement and low voices beyond his ability to make out. The flap was slowly moved aside, and the girl emerged. She was perhaps ten years old and appeared scared. She would not have been old enough to remember him from his time there.

"My grandmother says she remembers you," she said in Shoshoni. "She said you were a good boy, Buha's son. But you don't look like Buha. She said you brought me back from the bad men who stole me and my sisters when I was very young. I don't remember you."

Clay looked around. "Where is Buha? Where is my mother? Where is Eloo? Where is everybody?"

He spoke in English without thinking. The girl started to back into the opening, fearful of this fast-talking man who had hair both on his head and on his face. She had learned some English as had all the other children under the tutorage of Marta. But this man spoke too quickly, and she couldn't separate the words in her mind.

Clay realized his mistake and repeated his question in her language. She understood but didn't answer. The old woman eased painfully through the opening and shaded her eyes with withered hands to look up at him.

"The white man come. Many man. Soldier mans. But some not soldiers too.

Soldier man say they want to make peace. They bring sugar and flour. Buha say yes and he put his name on a piece of paper. Buha and the big chief of soldiers smoke together. Everybody happy because we not want to be part of war with white mans and Snake people.

"We mix flour with water when they left. It make us all sick. All sick. Warriors too sick to hunt. Women too sick to look for roots and berries. We stayed sick a long time. No one can eat. Most die. Huzi die, Eloo die, most children die. Then bad white men come. Same white men. But only four this time. Not soldiers. They say they come to trade but then they see how sick we are. They go through tepees killing all the men. They do bad things to women and girls and then kill them too."

She looked over at the girl, "She was at the water when the men came, and she heard screams and hid in the trees. I was too old. They leave me alone."

"What about my mother and father?"

"Marta tried to protect some of the girls and the man with the long red hair on his face hit her with his rifle and knocked her down. When she got back up he shot her in leg. Then he walked to her and looked at her close. He said something to other men and laughed and then tried to rip her clothes off. She fought with him and cut him with her knife on his arm. He yelled and jumped back and then shot her again. She died.

"Buha had not been sick like others and he come from hunting just as that man shot your mother. He ran to her and the man shot him in the leg. Then he walked over to him and shot him in the other leg. Still, Buha tried to get up. The man with the scar shot him in the back. He didn't die though. Then they tied ropes to each of his hands and feet and ran their horses in different directions. He died then."

With all the strength he had, Clay forced himself not to react. There would be time for that later.

"Are there any others alive?"

"Yes, they didn't hurt the little ones except for one boy that they ran over with horses and laughed about it as they rode away. I saw everything they did. We have four of our young women and three braves that survived after being left for dead. But everyone is afraid to go out. Maybe the whites will come back."

"How long ago?"

"The moon was just a sliver."

The moon was now nearly full. Weeks ago, thought Clay. Suddenly he knew he had to be alone.

"I'll be back before dark."

Walking down to the creek, then across the ice-cold water and into the pine trees beyond, he finally sat down on a fallen log and for the first time he could remember, cried in great heaving bursts that shook his entire being. The tears streamed down his face as he remembered so many times with his mother, Buha, Knife Thrower and Bow Shooter and his younger siblings. He thought of the times Buha's sister, Eloo, had taken him on long walks to learn the various birds and the sounds they each made. Something she loved. She also taught him about the edible plants and the ones that could be used as medicine. He thought about the hours and hours of being able to sit with his mother as she taught him the ways of the white man. She had told him over and over that he would someday need to know the white man's language and numbers and history. Of course, she had been right. He relived the hunting trips with his father, Buha, and the lessons that he insisted that his adopted son learn. The hours of practice each week with bow and arrow, knife throwing, club usage and hand to hand combat.

How he had been taught to ride a horse bareback with nothing but his knees to guide it. And the years of friendship with his two best friends that were always there for each other no matter what. And his little brother and sister that he had promised to tell all about the white man's world when someday he would return. No longer were they able to hear his stories.

How long he sat there he didn't know. The sobbing slowly subsided and the grief began to be replaced with anger and then hatred and then determination to find and kill the four men that had committed these horrific acts. He gathered himself, went to the creek and washed his face. When he returned to the tepee, he asked about the other survivors and went to see them one by one. He was thrilled to see that one of them was Knife Thrower. He and the other men were now able to stand for short periods of time but not much more. They were beginning to heal. Clay would stay to provide food and firewood until they were all strong enough to travel. He would also be there in case of any other trouble. They would then go to their winter grounds below. He was anxious to get on the trail of the men who had done this but knew he must wait. Buha had always told him that patience was the most important element of any hunt. So, he would wait.

The days slowly turned to weeks. He talked for hours with Knife Thrower and helped him regain his strength. He was not sure how Knife Thrower would react at the sight of any other white men in the future. His mother and sister had been among the murdered. He could tell Knife Thrower was filled with hatred and he made no attempt to talk against it. He himself felt the same way.

Finally, Knife Thrower and the others decided it was time to move his little tribe to the lowlands. They dismantled all the tepees and stacked them for future use. They would not be back to use them until the next summer, if, indeed they ever came back. The winter would be spent at the confluence of the Owyhee and Snake Rivers. Clay would not be staying with them.

Vengeance is Mine, and recompense;
Their foot shall slip in due time;
For the day of their calamity is at hand,
And the things to come hasten upon them.

Deuteronomy 32:35

The sun felt good on his back and he was glad to be back on the trail. These past few weeks, getting his people settled and hunting enough to provide their winter provisions had made him feel somehow trapped. At least the white men had not destroyed any of their food that had been gathered. The band would be very well equipped for the cold ahead.

A sensation of freedom and purpose had rewarded his departure. He had been told that a new town of whites had been established since he had been away. A place called Silver City. It was only about fifty miles back up in the high country. It was there that he hoped to find the killers of his family and friends. It would be his first and only mission until he tasted the satisfaction of revenge that burned inside his gut.

Clay had changed back into his white man garb and people of the town paid little attention to the young man that rode up to the Idaho Hotel and saloon. Many did, however, take note of the horse he rode. These were miners. Men who spent most of their time in the hot humidity of the mine tunnels that dotted the surrounding hills. Few had horses of their own. The remaining prospectors had mules but seldom rode them, using them instead as pack animals and walking just ahead of them. Most had once owned or at least ridden horses in their past and none had ever seen anything like Plato. Clay stepped down from the stirrup and tied each of the horses to a rail as a small crowd gathered to inspect the magnificent animal. Clay would have normally been receptive and very willing to brag about the horse. That friendliness had left him when he found out about his family. When his mother and father had died, somehow, something within him went with them. Normally known for his wit and quick laughter, now only a cloud of intensity and disinterest hung over him. He ignored questions and leaving the men to look over Plato, he walked up onto the boardwalk and into the front of the hotel. The man behind the counter just glanced up for a second before lowering his head to the newspaper he had laid out in front of him.

Without looking up again, he said, "Got one bed in a double room, that's all I got left.

Buck and a half, two bucks if you want a bath with it."

Now he looked up, taking in the young man that stood in front of him. What he saw was a tall, well-structured boy looking to be in his early twenties, long hair reaching below his shoulders, escaping from under a well-shaped and expensive beaver skin hat. The wide brimmed type that came out of Texas now that the war was over. The face was handsome, but rugged, full lips surrounded by a beard and mustache. And something else, the eyes, blue, focused, no nonsense, determined, hard. And an overall sadness it seemed. Then he noticed the Colt Navy resting quietly in a holster tied at the bottom around his thigh. He'd heard of men tying down their holsters to allow for a faster draw but had never seen anyone wearing an iron that way. As he recalled, it was more common in the cow country of Texas and the like. A leather hammer strap at the top of the holster was looped over to secure the gun while riding. This was often seen on the holsters of most who rode much. The Navy was a common weapon as well, made by

Samuel Colt's company and used widely throughout the war. This particular gun however was different. The wooden grips had been traded out for what appeared to be bone or even ivory. His pants were a tan, light weight material with a soft-looking rawhide seat sewn in, held up by a wide leather belt instead of suspenders as was typical. The shirt was a Mexican cotton but of obvious tailoring, open at the neck. The boy looked hard, but he definitely wasn't poor.

"You see a fellow around here with a long red beard?"

"Along with three other fellas?"

"That would be him, where are they?"

"Lacy Bernhardt. Three others with him but only Bernhardt signed in. Checked out a month ago but I seen em' in town every week or so since. I think they might be out prospectin' here bouts. Friends uh yourn?"

"What day do they usually come to town?"

"Like all the others, Saturday."

"What's today?"

"Why, today's Thursday. You been on the trail long?"

"A while, I'll take the room and the bath. You already rented out that other bed?"

"No sir, but I'm sure you'll get company tonight."

"I'll take both beds while I'm here. I don't want company."

"Well, that's double then."

"Minus a second bath, so that's three fifty, right?"

The clerk thought for a moment doing the calculation, "Well yes, it is."

Clay tossed the money on the counter and the man handed over a key.

"I'll take all three keys. The other guest key and your spare house key. I don't want any company, expected or otherwise."

"Well, we have a policy...."

He looked at Clay's eyes and decided the policy could be changed. Clay collected the three keys and, after depositing his belongings in the room, headed for the saloon. One of the other things he had become good at while at college was holding vast amounts of liquor. Drinking contests were a regular occurrence.

Clay had just walked up to the bar to order when a big miner approached the other end. Clay watched him in the huge mirror on the back bar.

Looking down at the miner, the barkeep said, "I'll be right with you Rake."

Turning back to Clay he said, "What can I get you young man?"

Before he could answer, Clay heard the big man at the far end of the bar.

"Better get him some sarsaparilla or maybe some milk."

Clay kept his eyes on the bartender, "I'll have a bottle of your best whiskey."

Just as he said that he recognized a brand he liked on the shelf of the back bar.

"In fact, that bottle right there will do just fine."

"Now Phil, don't be given that child that bottle. Or ifn ya do, ya might wanna put a nipple on it"

Clay continued to look at the bar keep and waited. He could see that the man was nervous. It was apparent that the big man was a bully, and this wasn't the first time he'd pushed people around here in the saloon.

"Forget that baby and come down here and serve a real man, Phil."

Clay could see the helplessness in Phil's eyes. Clay slowly turned to face the ruffian.

"I'm just here to get a bottle and go back to my room. Unfortunately for you, I arrived just a few seconds before you so I get served first. I know that, Phil understands that, if you're too stupid to see that, then I suggest you go get yourself some education."

He turned to Phil, "They got a grade school here in Silver City?"

"You bet, just over on the hillside there."

It had taken only that long for the miner to cover the ten feet between them.

He was already coming down toward Clay's head with one of his huge fists. It caught Clay a glancing blow that made him stumble several steps backwards, being held up only by a sliding grip on the bar.

The big man was at least three inches taller than Clay and outweighed him by a good fifty pounds. His size belied his speed. He was quick.

A kick in the side sent Clay over a table at the end of the bar. He had trouble catching his breath. He was surprised by the agility of his antagonist and he hurt. He didn't dare stay down.

Already the table was tossed to the side and he saw a size 14 boot coming toward his head. In desperation, he rolled clumsily to one side. The boot smashed down an inch beside his ear.

He continued to roll behind another table and with only seconds to spare, was able to regain his footing. Rake was not waiting. He was charging again, knocking everything in his way to the side.

This time, Clay was ready!

He sidestepped the lunge, jammed his boot into the side of the man's knee. He felt the crunch and the joint give. Getting a shove on his shoulders as he stumbled by, the man's momentum carried him crashing to the floor.

The cry of pain filled the establishment like a clasp of thunder.

In an instant, Clay had his Navy out, cocked and shoved into Rake's mouth, down his throat until he was gagging and choking.

Terror and shock were radiating from the miner. Looking up at Clay, he didn't move. Clay said nothing, staring back at Rake and still trying to clear his head and smooth out his breathing. A deep breath sent searing pain from a badly bruised rib. After a few seconds he spat some blood and pushed the barrel a bit deeper into the mouth.

"I can't stand fellas like you. You started this and I have every right to just blow your head off."

He was still trying to get his breath and the speech was an effort.

He glanced up at Phil, "What say, Phil. Should I just save everybody from this swine?"

Phil stood behind the bar with a slight smile on his lips but didn't answer.

"Well, Swine, Phil didn't really give me the go-ahead, so I guess you get to live for a bit longer. We'll see how you conduct yourself over the next couple minutes."

With that he pulled the gun back, stood up while trying not to show the pain that the effort brought forth, pulled a rag from the bar, wiped the end of his gun barrel and tossed the rag back.

"Throw that into your wash, Phil. It's got swine slobber all over it."

Clay stepped over Rake and back to the bar. Surveying the tables behind him in the mirror he saw at least a dozen men at various tables, sitting or standing like statues. Those who had the misfortune of knowing Rake could hardly believe what they were witnessing.

Slowly, Rake gathered himself enough to regain his footing, all the time holding his knee. He turned and looked at all the other men that were now staring at him.

"You think this means anything?" he cried out in his gruff but now shaky voice, "It don't mean a thing to all you midgets! I'll still skin all uh ya alive!"

He whirled around to face Clay. Even with his knee dislocated, he was ready to throw another haymaker. Instead, he caught two quick jabs to his nose and a chop to the side of his neck that took him right back to the floor. Writhing in pain and holding his broken nose with one hand and his knee with the other, he groaned and cursed. Clay put a foot on his neck and applied pressure.

"Ahhhg, you're killin me!"

"Well, that sure could be the case. Here's a thought Rake. Why don't you apologize to all these gentlemen and maybe you will get to walk out of here? What do you think?"

"Alright! Alright, just take your foot off of me."

Clay applied a little more weight.

"Hmmm. Nope, apology first."

Rake squirmed, trying to get loose. "Aagh! I'm agonna kill ya!"

"So... Do I take that to mean that we won't be getting an apology?"

He stepped down harder.

"Alright! I'm sorry, let me go!"

"That's better. Now, are you a man of your word, Rake?"

"Yes, please, it hurts bad, let me go. I can't hardly breathe!"

"Ok, one more thing, tell Phil and everybody else in here that you will never cause trouble again and that you'll act like a grown-up gentleman, so help you."

"Ahhhg, it hurts!"

"Rake? Need that promise."

"Yes, I promise."

"Promise what, Rake?"

"I promise never to cause no more trouble."

"And what else?"

"Ahhhg, I promise to be a gentleman damn you!"

"You did well, Rake, now get up, and go away. I don't want to see you again while I'm in town. Oh, and Rake, I will always be coming back through every so often after I leave this time. If I find out that you have been being your old self again... well, you know."

He took his foot off the neck and Rake stumbled up, back against the bar, holding his neck. Blood was pouring from his nose and was soaking his dirty shirt. Phil handed him a bar towel to keep him from bleeding all over everything. Rake quickly put it to his nose. He looked around and started to say something but thought better of it. With one last look at Clay, he limped out the door to the street. Laughter followed him as he made his exit.

Clay turned back to Phil.

"Can I have a glass to go with that bottle? Promise I'll bring it back."

Plato had been boarded at the livery that stood within sight of Clay's hotel window on the other side of the creek and on the next road over. Clay had rubbed down the horse and brushed him, talking softly to him the entire time. It had been a long time since the horse had been treated to oats and he gobbled them down with sheer pleasure. The stable keeper had been an eager buyer for the other horses and tack. The price was well below the going rate and with some good feed he figured he could resell the horses for a fine profit.

Finally, Clay patted the animal on its neck and gave the stable keeper an extra two bits to keep a close eye on the horse. He walked slowly back toward the Idaho Hotel. Along the way he stopped and ate his supper while listening to all the small talk taking place at the tables around him. The food was good and fairly priced. The teenage girl that served him was quick to keep his coffee cup full and bring his pie as soon as she saw him take his last bite of steak. At one point he caught a glimpse of a shapely woman of perhaps his own age in the kitchen area. He couldn't get a good look at her but thought she seemed to be running the place. He finished his pie and coffee, left money on the table, tipped his hat to the girl who was already clearing his dishes and headed across the street to his room.

The bottle, a third gone, with the upside-down-glass resting atop, sat on the washbasin table. Clay sat in the only chair, next to the window, his legs propped up on the edge of the bed. He studied the street below as the twilight faded to darkness. What had been a bustling throng of men, wagons and mules just two hours earlier had now dwindled to just the occasional passerby. The stores were closed leaving only the saloons open. He pulled his pocket watch out and noted 9:05. He had watched as the little café where he had taken his supper closed up and the pretty proprietor walked down the boardwalk. He thought about the story told him by Annie and Bert and how they had met when she was just newly started with the hotel café. He smiled at the memory. It had been only a few months since leaving them but Santa Fe seemed a world and a lifetime away. He took another look at the café. *The Eatery*. Good name.

There had been folks walking down the hallway, coming and going from their rooms all evening. The floor creaked each time a man's heavy work boots clomped a step and the click of a woman's high button shoes passed by his door. This time, he looked to the door with more interest. The creaking steps had stopped outside his door. He reached over to the bedpost and pulled the Navy from its holster. Other than that, he just sat quietly, listening and watching. The doorknob didn't move. Someone was just standing in the hall, trying to decide what to do. Finally, a tentative light knock. Clay moved slowly in his stocking feet without a sound. Even the floor didn't make any sound under his weight. Standing beside the door he said nothing. Again, the barely audible knock, knock, knock. It must be someone who wanted only for him to hear it. Or, maybe they were just checking to see if he was awake or in his room at all. Well, time to find out.

Still standing to one side, he grasped the knob, turned it and jerked open the door. It was Phil the bartender.

"Can I come in? I don't want anybody seeing me."

Clay thought for a second and then nodded. Phil came in, Clay checked both ways down the hall and closed the door.

"You won't need that," said Phil, looking at the Navy in Clay's hand.

Clay walked back to the bedpost, deposited the revolver in its holster and turned to face Phil.

"I know Phil is your given name, but I don't know your rightful name."

"It's Bannon."

"Very good Mr. Bannon, how can I help you?"

"I wanted to let you know that Rake Hamas is tellin' folks that he's gonna gun ya down. He's crazy to begin with but what you did to him today, in front of all them men, well, he's plum insane now. I just wanted you to know so's, if you're of a mind, you could git outta town afore he makes his move."

"I appreciate that Mr. Bannon. How will he likely do it?"

"Don't rightly know but you can bet it won't be straight up. He's killed two other men since he came here last fall. He picked a fight with old Ben Liesh at Barton's place and when old Ben made a swing at him he just let the old man hit him square in the jaw. Course, Old Ben didn't have no punch left in him and Rake just laughed and then proceeded to beat him near to death. Some men got Ben over to Doc's, but he died the next day. Doc said his brain swelled up to where it was ready to explode.

Then there was George Hayley. He had a claim up Lost Gulch a mile or so outta town. He came in for supplies and Rake offered to buy into the claim. George declined but that didn't satisfy Rake. A few days later, George came into town again, all bruised up on his face and signed a paper saying he sold a one fourth interest to Rake. George had been a tough old prospector, and this was his first producer. He was getting' nearly 18 cents outta it and said he was just gettin to the good stuff. He wouldn't have sold to the good Lord himself. But he was scared when I saw him that day. We all knew that Rake or one of his thugs had beat him bad."

"What happened to him that he's dead?"

"I'm gettin to it. George went back to the mine and went back to work. Rake never left town to help out at the mine but sure did take a share of every ounce George brought into the assay office. George finally had had enough and confronted Rake in the saloon. Said Rake had never given him the money for his share and never did a lick of work and he was a dirty thief. Said he was done giving Rake anything. Well, Rake's known for his gun work and George never carried one of his own. Rake just calmly asked just what it was that George thought he was thinking about to call him a thief and George best be ready to back up words like that. Rake reached down and loosened his gun in that fancy holster he wears. George said he didn't have no gun, or he would sure nuff take on Rake. Rake nodded to Lester Guild, one of his trash friends and Lester pulled out his gun and tossed it to George. George caught it with his left hand and looked shocked and confused about what to do. He looked up at Rake and out of desperation switched it to his right hand just as Rake drew his gun and shot George in the belly. George fell but held onto the gun. He tried to raise himself up and Rake shot him right between the eyes. Pure murder if ya ask me."

"Why wasn't he arrested?"

"Sheriff was downright afraid of him. Rake had him buffaloed. The townsfolks were so upset with the sheriff that he resigned and hightailed back to the valley. He had two deputies, but they pulled stakes with him."

"How about the new sheriff?"

"Ain't got one yet. Had a constable but he said his job was to handle the small stuff. Not no murders and such. He just left last week so we ain't got no law at all right now.

The council wrote to the governor asking for some temporary help but ain't heard nothin back yet."

"Town this size should be settling down by now. How long's it been a town?"

"Well, the Jordan party hit color in the spring of '63. Came over from the Boise Basin strike of '62 lookin for the Blue Bucket. You heard of that?"

Clay shook his head.

"Well, legend says a lost wagon train came through these mountains and found nuggets so big and plentiful that they used 'em for fishing weights. Winter was comin' on so they hung up a blue water bucket to mark the spot and moved on. Don't know what happened that they never came back but they didn't. Fact is, nobody rightly knows if that find actually exists and if it does if it's even in these mountains. Anyway, Michael Jordan's bunch didn't find the Blue Bucket but I'm thinking they sure did hit it just as big with what they did find. They set up a town down the creek. That's Ruby City, you been there?"

Clay shook his head again.

"Don't make no difference. Not much left there no more. 'Bout half a mile and on the other side of the creek. Up on the hillside.

"Well, as things kept movin' up the creek, it's called Jordan Creek after the man that led them propectors, some of the folks started buildin' shacks and such and began calling it Ruby City. By the time the first year came and went there was so many prospectors and all the scum that come following them, that there wasn't enough room in Ruby. So, they came up the creek here and over time moved most all the buildings up here. Even this hotel. In pieces of course. Pulled the pieces on rough sleds over the snow. Must be a couple thousand people here now. Even got us a newspaper. Well, I gotta be gittin back. Just wanted to let you know."

He stood up from the chair he'd been occupying and started for the door.

"Rake won't go easy," he said as he briefly turned halfway around.

"I thank you for your warning and information," Clay replied as he opened the door, looked both ways in the hall and then nodded for Phil to take his leave.

Saturday morning was clear and bright. Clay awoke with great anticipation. He hadn't been able to learn anything of value as to where Red Beard might be in the hills, so he was stuck with waiting for Saturday when the desk clerk and several others had told him they most often came to town. He found that the four killers of his parents preferred the First Place Saloon directly across from his hotel. He had also learned that the four all rode bays with black tails. Typically, they would be trailing at least one mule. They weren't friendly to the locals but hadn't caused much trouble either. A little loud when drinking, which was most of the time when they were in town, but that was about it. They all bragged about what great Indian killers they had been before turning to mining. Red Beard carried a tobacco pouch that he claimed was made from the skin of an Indian he killed.

Clay dressed, shaved and went across the street to find some breakfast. The run-ins with the three desperados that he had been forced to shoot down, combined with his confrontation with Rake, had somehow added a lot of maturity. While he was wary of other men, he felt no fear. He remembered listening to a conversation between Bert and Rand one time. Rand had said something about not fearing any man alive. Bert had chuckled and said the day would come when some man, somewhere, would put the pure fear of the Lord in him. He said the lack of experience of the young gave that feeling of invincibility. He said that will change with age and time. Well, it hadn't happened to Clay yet.

He ate eggs, bacon, fried spuds and a third of a loaf of fresh baked sour dough bread. He took his last cup of coffee with him out the door to the boardwalk.

He hadn't seen Rake since that incident but knew he was still around. He really didn't care. He was in Silver City for just one reason. "Red Beard" Lacy Bernhardt, and his three friends. Nobody seemed to know the rightful names of the other three. Not that they would use their given names anyway. Most of their type had numerous aliases.

Silver City, Idaho was typical of mining camps. It had taken only weeks after the first pan showed color before those first 29 or 30 prospectors were joined by hundreds and then thousands of others spreading out over a hundred square miles of rugged mountains. The mining camps, as did Silver City, always followed the same pattern. First were the original prospectors, in this case, a group led by a man named Michael Jordan who unfortunately soon ran crossways of some hostiles and died of his wounds.

For a few days or even weeks, the original discoverers would have their opportunity to stake their pick of the claims, set up rules and name the creeks, gullies, and surrounding mountains if they so desired. Many would even take the time to lay out a town and in addition to their ore claims, take ownership of the lots in the coming town. Most had been through it before and knew they would be joined shortly with the throngs of gold seekers. Setting up the town site and selling the lots could finance a good start to their own mining endeavors.

Along with the prospectors looking for gold and silver would come the second wave. The people who prospected not for gold from a claim but for the gold in the miner's pockets. First in a new camp would be the pack mules with cheap whiskey. The early saloon might be just a couple of rough-cut planks placed atop anything that would hold them. Sometimes kegs, sometimes just a few rocks stacked up and covered with a good-sized tent. Most likely the owner would sleep right there in the tent to protect his stash of libations.

No saloon could last long without a card table or two. The card tables brought the card sharks. A few, because they were very good at their craft, were honest, but the most common was the slight-of-hand kind. They worked from one camp to another until their reputation caught up with them and nobody would sit at their table. Then they would move on.

Next came the soiled doves who tried to set up shop as close to the busiest saloon as possible. Within several more weeks came the more legitimate businesses. The stores, the cafes, the blacksmiths, the assay office, makeshift hotels, carpenters. And from the very beginning, the men who stole, murdered and swindled. The likes of Rake Hamas and Lacy Bernhardt.

Most all these early comers stayed for only short periods of time. Always though, the likes of Rake Hamas and Red Beard would try to intimidate their way into running the towns. Taking over through threats and killing. If they weren't stopped early on, they would control the town. The exceptions came if the strike was very large and attracted the big mining operations with outside bank money that came in to develop deeper shafts with huge crews. At that point, some would move on to the next strike knowing they couldn't outgun the talent these huge operations could finance. More than one big fish in a small pond found themselves looking at professionals, like the Pinkertons, among other lesser known but equally effective organizations for hire. The big money boys were not above hiring some of the deadliest of gunmen and in numbers beyond the reach of even the most dedicated of the roving, small time bullies.

On the other hand, the big boys often could have cared less about what went on in the streets of the mining town if it didn't interfere with their day-to-day mining operations. Therefore, lowlifes like Rake Hamas could survive. They picked on the businesses who served the miners but rarely the miners themselves. They walked a fine line, trying not to openly break the law in such a manner as to attract the state or federal authorities.

Now, since Lincoln's war was over, more troops were in the west to protect the growing population from Indians. And state or territorial troops were available to be called in if a town got too out of hand. The ruffians were dependent on being able to buy off or intimidate the local lawmen. Often, they would muscle their way into being the law themselves. Ultimately, if all worked well, they would end up owning the most productive of businesses. If they couldn't do that, they would take a share of the earnings in exchange for supporting illegal practices while looking the other way.

Now, Clay Brackett was witnessing some of that.

Lacy Bernhardt bragged about his many personal victories during the War Between the States. Stroking his long red beard, he detailed each event with the showmanship of a stage actor. Enough acts of heroism that it seemed he had been at every major battle and many more that his listeners had never heard of. That Bernhardt was good with a gun was not in dispute. He often demonstrated his expertise by shooting tin cans and bottles. Although few had ever seen a real gunman's quickness and accuracy with a handgun, it seemed that Bernhardt's demonstrations showed that he had both abilities. That he could kill with great willingness and even enjoyment, was also without question. The three men that traveled with him bore witness to that. The little band took great pleasure in bragging about how they had single handedly wiped the earth clean of a hundred Indians earlier that very year. They failed to mention that most had already died of sickness or were in the last throws of death and unable to defend themselves.

These, the Indians they bragged about killing were the Mountain Shoshonis. The band that had raised Clay Brackett.

Most of the wartime achievements attributed to Lacy Bernhardt were in fact true. They could be verified in numerous news reports of the day. What only Jerome Langley knew was that he, Langley had shot the real Lacy Bernhardt in the back as he camped with an old prospector near the Boise Basin.

The real Lacy Bernhardt had left his Captain's position with the defunct rebel army and, alone, discouraged and hoping for a fresh start, had come west to try his hand at prospecting. He arrived in the Boise Basin with the only person he had run across on the trail those last few days. An old man who had spent the last forty years trying to find his own personal strike. They had talked and found they were amenable to working together. Coming across a likely spot to try some panning, they made camp late in the day and scooped up some gravel from the stream. The old prospector gave a hoot and showed Bernhardt a bit of color. It was just then that Jerome Langley happened by and saw the little celebration. He watched as the two pulled out pan after pan of excitement-causing ore flakes. When darkness came, he simply walked up and shot both as they sat eating their supper. Going through the two dead men's belongings he discovered the identity of Lacy Bernhardt and the several news clippings that he carried with him. Plenty of information for Jerome Langley to build a story around. His own name on several wanted posters, he decided to take the name as his own. His three partners came into his life weeks later and had no idea that he wasn't the hero he claimed to be. It was part of the reason they allowed him to lead them.

Clay was up early. He had been told that Bernhardt on occasion had come in within an hour or two of sunrise. He sat in front of the café sipping the coffee and alternately whittling on a willow stick. His Navy Colt rested easily in its holster. The tie-down strings hung loose for comfort. His hat was tilted slightly forward to keep out the morning sun. A slight whirlwind kicked up dust down the street. Behind the café, a magpie complained loudly about a yelping dog on the opposite hillside. Up on the big mountain known as War Eagle, a few sticks of dynamite gave forth with a muffled explosion. The miners had claimed a few more feet of tunnel. Across the opposite corner, a tall, slender man of sixty, with a long white apron, swept dust and dirt out the front door of the general store. A brown-headed boy came running by chasing a hoop. The hoop, taller than the boy, rolled ahead, nudged along with a stick he carried. Clay smiled as he remembered the many games of his childhood. It would have been great to have one of those hoops to chase with Bow Shooter and Knife Thrower. Of course, they had no idea of such.

He caught a glimpse of them while they were still up the gulley, a quarter mile away.

Four mounted men leading a mule. They went in and out of sight as they methodically worked their way down to the upper street of town. Between buildings he caught glimpses until they reached the cross street that led to the corner where he sat. The red beard was obvious, and Clay's heart raced. The men dismounted in front of the hotel, tied off the horses and the mule and went into the saloon. Clay, trying to calm himself, slowly rose, laid down the willow stick and tied the holster string around his leg. This was the moment he had been waiting for. Now, he didn't know exactly how he would engage the four murderers. He couldn't just walk in and shoot them. Or could he? He could feel the hatred rising quickly. He was about to cross the street when two men rode up and tied their horses to the hitching rail just down from the mule.

Rake and his buddy! This would complicate things. Six men that would all want to kill him as soon as he made his move. The Navy held five cartridges. He knew Rake held himself out to be tough but had heard very little about his gun skills. More than likely he used his brute strength a lot more than the gun he carried on his hip. The gun was worn high, not in a good drawing position. The most likely challenge would be from Lacy Bernhardt. He wore his gun a bit lower but not tied down. He was evidently quite good at target shooting but could he hold up against another man? Somehow Clay didn't think so. He talked too much, bragged too much. Most often, big talkers didn't have the metal to keep up with their big mouths. The three men with him looked rough and capable. They wore guns but not in quick draw position. The fellow with Rake looked to be half-witted but he carried a scatter gun in his left hand. That might be the deal breaker. You didn't have to be fast or accurate if you had a short-range blaster like that.

The mule brayed as Clay crossed the street to the saloon entrance. When he walked through the door all six were sitting together at a table toward the back. It figured that they would know one another. As human beings, they were peas in a pod.

The table was under the stairway and it took Clay a few seconds to let his eyes adjust. They and he were the only patrons. It was early in the day. Phil was behind the bar polishing glasses and when Clay walked up and put one foot on the rail, Phil gave a slight nod toward the table. Clay just winked with an air of confidence he didn't really feel. For just a few seconds, the conversation at the table stopped and then resumed in lower voices. His eyes had adjusted and when he turned around with his back to the bar, he looked right at the killers. They were already looking at him.

It was Rake that spoke first.

"Well, well, looky thar boys. It's that smarty pants kid. He caught me on an off day but I'm all better now and I think I will just kill him right where he stands."

With that all six stood up and began to spread out with about two feet separating each of them.

"Good to see you Rake," Clay smiled easily, "I'm like you, I just didn't feel like we understood each other. Also, you need to know that you're keeping very poor company.

That red bearded son-of-a-bitch beside you and his pig friends are murderers. They killed my mother and her husband in cold blood. Now, Rake, you need to think this through. I am going to kill them, but you got a chance to run if you want. Just don't come back."

The look on Lacy Bernhardt's face was one of disbelief.

"What are you talkin' about? I killed some Indians but not no white woman and man."

"Those Indians were my family. They were sick or had already died and all the stories you been telling are lies. The man you ripped apart with horses was the man that raised me. His wife was my mother. And she was as white as I am. Now's the time you pay for it."

Lacy Bernhardt didn't wait. He went for his gun and the little man with the scatter gun started to pull it up, too. Bernhardt yelled, "Get him Max!" and shot first. His bullet went a foot wide of Clay who was already moving. Clay shot him in his gun arm, and he let out a grunt and rolled onto the floor.

His gun fell three feet away. Clay never hesitated. He hit the floor on a roll and came to a prone position with both hands holding his revolver with outstretched arms. The next shot went straight into the man with the shotgun as he fired off one of the two barrels. The discharge went ten feet high as he yelped, took about three steps toward Clay and fell dead. Rake had his gun out and was firing as fast as he could cock and pull the trigger. Just as Clay had hoped, Rake was no gunman and the bullets were hitting all over the place but not in Clay. One of Bernhardt's men was more levelheaded and was taking calm aim. The bullet crashed into the floor right beside Clay's head sending wood splinters into the side of his forehead. He rolled again and put his next shot squarely between the man's eyes. The one they called The Mex was shooting and coming close with each shot, Clay rolled back the other way just avoiding the man's lead. The other man, Max, saw what was happening and made a dash for the door. Bernhardt had scooted to his gun and picked it up with his left hand, aiming at Clay just as Clay saw Rake running toward him.

Clay put two shots in the big man's heart and turned to shoot Bernhardt. *Click*! The Navy was empty.

Bernhardt realized what had happened and began to laugh. Grinning like a crazy man, his right arm limp and dripping blood, he pulled up and shot once but missed. Pulling himself to a sitting position he said, "Yeah, now I remember, your ma was right good lookin'. Too bad she was up with that stinkin' Indian."

Clay ran directly toward him, watching until the revolver was aimed at him and then dove to the floor. He rolled toward the scatter gun and, finding it only a body length from Bernhardt, felt a slug rip into his thigh. Pulling the double barrel into position, he cocked both hammers and not knowing which barrel had been fired, pulled both triggers at once. Bernhardt had only time to register surprise before his midsection exploded, knocking him into the side of the staircase and the table legs where he had been sitting just seconds before.

Clay used the shotgun as a crutch to lift himself into a chair beside Bernhardt. The man was looking up at the ceiling.

"I didn't plan on dyin' this mornin'. Just came in for a drink."

With those last words he coughed up some blood and stopped breathing. Clay studied him for a moment with the realization that compared to the blood that dripped through it, the man's beard hadn't been red at all. Just a rusty orange.

He was trying to look at his leg through the blood flowing into his eye. The room seemed to explode in a single gunshot. He twisted in his chair to see Phil standing behind the bar, a smoking Colt Army .44 in his extended hand.

Clay looked toward the door and saw Max laying halfway inside, halfway outside. He looked back to Phil.

"Well, I didn't want to interfere with your fight, but I don't tolerate back shooters." Phil grinned, "That fella was fixin' to do just that."

"Thanks, I owe you one. Where did you learn to shoot like that?"

"Oh, we all got our stories I reckon. I'd like to hear yours, I ain't never seen nobody shoot like you."

A voice from out on the boardwalk, "You all done shootin' in there?"

"Yeah, Doc, come on in. We got one that could use some help."

The leg healed but the scar on his forehead above the left eye would be with him for the rest of his life. The three-inch piece of flooring that had blasted its way into the skin had to be cut out and stitched up. A reminder. Although he had no idea when it happened, he had taken a bullet through the flesh of his armpit. It was nasty and bled badly. He'd been lucky. The slug in his leg had missed everything vital and passed all the way through. It hurt but he could still make it to and from the outhouse without help. The armpit and head gashes were painful as well, but minor. As much as he hated to admit it, he knew he was going to be gimpy for a while.

PART FIVE

1865

He spent the first few days mainly in his room. She brought him breakfast that first one. She introduced herself as Bethany Alexander, owner of The Eatery, but he could call her Miss Alexander. That was the first time he saw her laugh. She then said she was just joking and that he could call her Beth.

At first, he didn't think too much about her. As the days went by, he began to realize that she was not only efficient but also prettier than he first thought. That realization happened the first time he hobbled down the stairs, through the lobby, onto the boardwalk, across the dirt street and finally flopped down in a chair at the closest table. She came from the back. It was the first time he had seen her with her long hair down. Blonde, like his mother's. It had always been in a bun before. It transformed her, at least in his mind.

"Well, well, look at you. What are you doing over here? You shouldn't be putting stress on that leg."

"Yes mother."

She laughed, "Well, somebody obviously needs to look after you."

She returned with a steaming cup of coffee and a plate of food.

"I was just getting ready to bring this over to you at the hotel. Hope you like steak and potatoes."

"Hmmm, doesn't look like steak to me."

"Didn't say it was, just said I hoped you liked it. I'm supposed to get a delivery of beef Monday but for now you'll have to settle for mutton. Spuds are real though."

She set a plate of bread next to him and a bowl of freshly churned butter. Going back into the kitchen, she returned with her own cup of coffee and sat down across the table from him.

A smile broke out as he took in hers.

"How old are you?" she asked.

"In years or life lived?"

Again, she laughed. It came easy for her. He liked it a lot.

"In years," she said.

"I was born 21 years ago last Thursday. How about you?"

"Well, happy birthday. I'm almost 20 years of age. I took over this place six months ago when my father got sick. He died two months ago and my mother died when I was 15 while we were on our way west."

"I'm sorry to hear that. How are you getting along?"

"Well, at least I don't have anyone trying to kill me like some people I could mention."

He winced, "Ow! That hurt more than my leg does."

A bit of a smile, "Sorry, I guess that wasn't all that funny. I get along fine. I sure miss my pa, uh, father, but he sold the house when he knew he was dying and made arrangements for me to live with the Richardsons, a nice couple that have that big house up the hill below the Rickshaw Mine.

He made enough off the house to make sure I would be financially able to relocate if I choose and make a new start. Haven't needed it so far because this place seems to more than take care of my small needs. Ellie comes in before and after school to help me out. Her daddy can only work in the mine a few hours a day because he has consumption. Her mother is kinda confused you might say, has a hard time with nearly everything. Nice as can be but just needs to stay home unless Ellie or Mister Evans is with her. So, Ellie works hard to help out. She and her father came in one day and said I was paying her too much and they couldn't take charity even though they sure appreciated my caring about them. I told them they were mistaken. I let them know that in my mind I was under paying her because she brought back so much business with her friendly and efficient work. I said I wouldn't know what to do without her and that's the real truth. And, well, I'm talking way too much. What about you, tell me everything and then what will you do now?"

All the dishes had been cleared away and Beth had propped open the door to let in the fresh air. They had continued to talk and Clay had told her a brief version of his life and the wagon train raid and his years growing up with the Shoshonis and how he had stayed with the Morgan family and come to love and respect them. He talked about how Rand Morgan and he went to college and how he was like a brother and his best friend and how Rand had taught Clay to fast draw and shoot with a handgun. He told her how Bert Morgan had taught him so much about dealing with white men who wanted to do harm and how his Indian father had taught him about the Indian way of surviving and fighting. Finally, he told her about losing his mother and adopted father and his Shoshoni family and why he had come to Silver City. She fought back tears as he went through the hard times in his life. And yet, she knew that he had left out much of the details that were just too hard for him to share with anyone.

"As for what comes next, I don't really know for sure. Thinking about riding over to that Camp Lyons. See if those army boys need a scout. Either that, or I might just head back up into the mountains that I grew up in. About twenty miles from here as the crow flies. Guess I'll hang around here until I'm walking better. At least another week or so.

It was ten days later, the leg still a bit tender but fully usable, sitting at The Eatery for his first meal of the day and talking with Beth when the door opened and a youngster of maybe 10 walked in and up to his table.

"Mr. Brackett?"

"That would be me."

"Mr. Brackett, I been sent to fetch you over to the mayor's barber shop. Him and the city council would like to talk with you. Oh, I was told to say for you to come ifn you were alright to do that. They wanted me to be all, uh, uh, respectful and such."

"What's your name friend?"

Raising to his full height and straightening his previously slumped shoulders, the boy said, "Why, I'm Jackson Hamilton Church the second, sir, but mostly they call me Rusty cuz uh my rusty colored hair."

"Well, Mr. Church, would you mind taking a message back to the mayor for me?"

"No sir, I mean yes sir, I'd be happy to."

Clay and Beth tried to keep a straight face.

"Thank you, Mr. Church, please use your very finest respect when you convey my answer..."

"Scuse me, what does that word convey mean?"

"When you tell them my answer. Tell them that I am involved in an important dinner meeting right now but would be happy to meet with them this afternoon. Tell them that I would be honored to have the pleasure of their company here at The Eatery or in the hotel lobby later today. Can you remember all that?"

"I think so."

He turned to go but Clay stopped him. He reached into his shirt pocket and extracted a quarter.

"This is for doing such a good job of relaying the messages and returning here with their answer."

"Wow! Wow! Two bits just for running down the street a couple times? Wow! Thank you!"

With that he was off on his errand. They watched him go and then looked at each other and broke into laughter.

"Eat your dinner," she chuckled, "I'll be back with some more coffee."

They talked while he ate his mutton stew, a second helping of potatoes and two big slices of buttered bread. Before he finished his pie, Rusty returned.

"They said that if you can wait until he finishes the haircut and shave he's aworkin on, they'll come right on over... Sir."

"Alright. Hey, how about we drop the formalities, forget being so proper I mean? How about you call me Clay and I call you Rusty? That be alright with you?"

"Oh, yes sir, I mean Clay."

"Alright, then Rusty, would you mind going back and telling them that I will wait for them here?"

"I sure will do that."

"Oh, and Rusty, one more thing," he pulled out a nickel and held it out between his thumb and index finger, "when you're done with that chore, go get yourself five pieces of hard candy at the store."

He belted out, "Yes sir!" His grin stretching the limits of his cheeks.

He turned to hurry out and then stopped and looked back, "I mean Clay." Giggling, he sped out the door.

There were five of them when they walked in. The two wearing hats took them off in deference to Beth and politely acknowledged her. She excused herself saying she had work to get to in the back and would let them visit. They introduced themselves one at a time. He had already met Henry Pelzer, the constable. Pelzer had come to talk with everyone at the saloon right after the shootings. Phil had told how Clay had been forced to defend himself and Clay backed up Phil on his shooting of the last one that tried to back-shoot Clay. Pelzer happily closed the inquiry and moved on.

Clay also knew Doc Simpson who had been keeping an eye on him and his wounds. He didn't recognize the other three.

Neil James

Henry Pelzer made the introductions, "This here is Drew Bongenhielm. Drew is our barber and mayor. This tall drink of water is Harv Fitwell, Harv and his brother Jan run the hardware store over on Washington Street. This fella here is Jackson Church, he runs the Jordan Creek Press, one of our newspapers."

They shook hands all around with Clay repeating each surname in turn. At the introduction of Church, he hesitated and smiled.

"I believe I've had the pleasure of meeting young mister Church the second a bit earlier."

Church grinned with pride, "Yes sir, that's my boy alright. He's a handful sometimes but I believe I'll hold on to him."

"I believe that's a good choice. Now gentlemen, how may I be of service?"

At this point Drew Bongenhielm took the lead, "As you may know, we are currently without a marshal. We had one but he fell out of favor and pulled up stakes."

Clay looked at Pelzer questioningly. Pelzer was quick to answer the look.

"I take care of legalities. Serving of notices and summons and such. I keep order in court. I sign off on lawsuits and carry out court orders. Claiming foreclosed property and the like. I do not deal with crimes. Especially crimes involving weapons. Don't get me wrong. I served in the war and even got a couple medals but I'm no gunman and I'm no fighter. I know my limits. I made a promise to my wife when I took this position and it's in my paperwork with the city."

Clay nodded and looked back at the mayor.

Bongenhielm continued, "That's exactly right. We have so many lawsuits over claim boundaries and such and paperwork has to go to Boise much of the time. We couldn't get by without him. Probably should pay him more but don't tell him I said that."

Everybody laughed. Clay thought to himself that these were the kind of men he liked. He would listen.

"Well, back to the Marshal position, it has been suggested several times by several citizens that we, the city council, approach you about taking on the job." He quickly added, "Just as a temporary position you understand. Just until we could get an election put together. Now the last marshal, the one that just left, we paid him forty-five dollars a month plus two meals per day when he was on duty. Uh, we understand that may not have been quite equitable and we are willing to pay you, for your temporary service, fifty-five a month and three meals per day. Just a way of opening the discussion you understand. We're open to suggestions."

"Yes indeed, we're certainly open to suggestions," chirped in Pelzer.

Clay was stunned. He had expected the visit to be a nice way of inviting him to leave their town and not come back. He sat there looking without expression from man to man.

"So, what do you say Mr. Brackett?" Pelzer finely broke the silence.

Clay cleared his throat, "Uh, you gentlemen know that I just turned twenty-one years old, right?"

They gave quick glances at one another before Doc Simpson spoke, "Look Clay, I've spent several hours with you. We know you're young. I also know that you have experienced more in your young life than most men twice your age. I hope it is alright that I shared some of what you told me with these fellas."

Clay shrugged as if to say that it was a bit late to ask now. Doc cleared his throat and went on.

"We all know that you are cool under fire, that you focus on what you want and I believe you are mature in judgement beyond your years. I was the first to suggest you for the job and I stand by it."

"Can I have a day or two to think about it?"

It was the mayor that jumped right in, "Oh, of course, this is a big decision, take all the time you need. Well, maybe not too long." He grinned and stood up reaching his hand out to shake.

The others followed suit. The last was Doc Simpson.

"Doc, could I have a minute?"

Doc sat back down as the others walked through the open door and into the street.

"Doc, thanks for staying. I need to ask a few questions that I just want to ask of you."

"I'll answer as best I can."

"I took a couple years of law in college, but I don't know all the local stuff out here. Are there books? Law books around here?"

"Judge Haines has a whole library over in Boise City. The only ones I know of other than some of the lawyers down in the valley. You got any yourself?"

"Back in Santa Fe at Bert Morgan's place. I guess I could get him and Annie to send them to me but that would take weeks. How often does a judge make it through here?"

"Oh, once a month unless something comes up that we need him sooner. Major stuff like murders or robbery and such, he'll make a special trip for."

The conversation continued for another half hour with Beth coming and going, refilling coffee cups and taking care of other customers. Phil stopped by for just a few minutes and agreed to meet up with Clay a little later that day. Clay wanted to get his opinion as well. After Doc left, Beth sat down again.

"Well, that all sounded, uh, intense."

Clay filled her in on the conversations.

"What do you think, Beth?"

"Well, of course it's not my life and limb on the line. I can tell you that those fellas you had to deal with the other day are not the only ones of their kind. There are and will be others. Mining towns are not like what I've heard about cow towns in Kansas and Texas. These are not just cowboys, kids really, blowing off steam. These men are here for money and some care little about what they do to get at it. It will mean using your gun again. Maybe again and again, are you ready for that?"

Clay thought long and hard about that. When Phil finished his daytime shift, he sat with Clay in the hotel lobby and they discussed what Phil had observed in the two years he had been in the town. As they talked, Clay took in the surroundings, four fabric covered chairs that looked to be of eastern vintage with colorful floral patterns. A bit worn but still in good useable condition.

The lobby itself was perhaps twenty feet wide and half again as long. The ceiling was of roughhewn boards cut from pine. He idly wondered where it came from having seen no such trees while coming to or staying in Silver City. The walls were covered with wallpaper in an Egyptian influence. The floor was of the same wood as the ceiling with a huge floral rug in the center. For an operation so far removed from big cities, the proprietors had done a fair job of decorating. Three side-by-side windows let light stream in from the street beyond and three more offered the same at the rear wall. Little dust particles danced in the shafts of fading sunlight. On the side away from where they sat was an arched doorway that invited guests into the attached saloon where the shooting had taken place. From time to time, Phil glanced in to make sure the evening bartender wasn't being overwhelmed. Twice he excused himself to step in for a few minutes to help until things slowed and he returned to their conversation.

The picture Phil painted was one of rough men with a desperate need to find gold and silver. Most were willing to work for it while fewer, but always present, were the ones willing only to take what wasn't theirs.

Between Indians, mine accidents and white men like Rake Hamas and Lacy Bernhardt, over thirty men had lost their lives just in the few years since the first color was discovered down the creek. Clay thought for a moment about that, six of those men had fallen to his gun and he was but twenty-one years old. Did he have it in him to risk killing more men? The thought didn't disturb him as much as he thought it should. And yet, he felt a deep concern for those people, young and old, whatever their color, that wanted nothing more than to live their lives in peace and work for what they earned. He was learning about himself more every day. He had little qualms about erasing from the earth those who preyed on the ordinary, everyday people just trying to get by.

Phil finished their conversation by suggesting that Clay could give it a try.

"Ya know yer not chained to the job. If'n ya don't like it after a few days or weeks, hell, just walk away. Town won't be no worse off'n they are now." He stood up, "Somethin to think about. I better git in there, Buddy's not able to keep up. He's a good kid but he's got a bit a learnin to do yet. Let me know what ya decide."

"I will, and thanks Phil"

Early the next day he took Plato from his stall and headed up Jordan Creek to Long Gulch and into the higher mountains beyond. Once out of sight of the town he stopped behind a rock fall. He stashed the saddle and bridle where they wouldn't be seen. He took off his shirt and boots and hat and pulled his moccasins from the saddle bags. For just a while he wanted to be one of Buha's tribe again. He just wanted to feel what it was to be a Mountain Shoshoni. With no tack other than just a length of rope looped around his neck; Plato must have felt the freedom too because he pranced out with abandon at Clay's slightest hint.

The day was bright and the air crisp. Great white clouds loomed in the distance as they drifted lazily to the east but showed no hint of moisture. From the highest peak he could make out the town far below to the north and see South Mountain off the opposite way. Part of him just wanted to keep on going. And why shouldn't he?

He understood the needs of some of the Indians to defend themselves and their hunting grounds. But he felt no kinship with them because other than a few days of trading once or twice a year when he was a boy, he had almost no contact with them. Although he had no memory of Great Bear, he knew the stories that had been passed down by Buha and others about how the tribe had come to be. He knew that they were considered outcasts by the other tribes because Great Bear had brought them from the Comanche nation.

He also felt nothing for the miners and other whites that sought to run the tribes from their ancestral lands. In the end, he decided he really had no allegiance to any group and no group of people held a passion for him. Their fights were not his fights and he wanted no part in them.

337

He wanted to someday see Knife Thrower again to see if he had found peace. He wondered how his childhood friend would judge him in white man clothes if push came to shove. He took a deep breath and slowly turned the war horse in a complete circle. The only connection he felt in this world was Plato and... and the young woman at The Eatery. That sudden realization surprised him.

When he walked into the barber shop, Drew Bongenhielm was just shaking the hair off of his last customer's cape. The man paid and left.

"Good to see you Clay, have you been thinking about our offer?"

"Little else Mayor. If the offer's still on the table I would be willing to give it a try. The forty-five a month will be fine. I don't need any more than what you've been paying. I'd like three meals a day though, say five days a week? I'm not much of a cook. That would be most often at The Eatery."

"That sounds more than fair to me. Anything else?"

"Oh, what about a deputy? I believe you said the last marshal had one."

"Yep, you can hire a deputy, thirty a month and meals when on duty. We'll give an extra fifteen a month for a part timer, too. If everything else sounds fine, then we're glad to have you."

"When do you want me to get going?"

"I got a badge right here in this drawer and I have the goods to swear you in right here and now. Papers come out tomorrow and we'll make sure your appointment is front page."

"Well, I guess that'll work. I didn't even ask, is there a jail?"

"Yes sir, we got ourselves one whale of a jail! Right up on the hillside across the creek. I can show you the way and open it up for ya. By the way, about the deputy, got anybody in mind?"

"Maybe, haven't asked yet."

That was the way it all started. Clay became the *Sheriff* of Silver City as he figured that a true *marshal* would be a federally appointed position such as held by Bert Morgan in Santa Fe. The irony of how Bert Morgan had become the law in Santa Fe wasn't lost on him. He chuckled when he mailed a letter telling the Morgan family about his new venture. He had told them about his mother and the Shoshonis and his run in with their killers in the saloon. A second letter followed just ten days later. At the end of it he put a short postscript:

"Oh, one more thing, the young lady that runs the best of the town's cafes is beautiful, smart and has a great smile and laugh. Her name is Beth. Reminds me of Annie. Maybe I'll marry her.... to be continued."

Sheriff Clay Brackett found his part time deputy behind the bar at the saloon. It was Phil. It turned out that Phil had been a sharpshooter in the war and was quite handy with a hand gun as well. Phil found a good fit between spending part of his time as bartender at the saloon and part as a deputy sheriff. Working at the bar gave him ears on things that might otherwise not be known to him and Clay. It was a lot of hours for Phil, but he was young and single and seemed to be totally dedicated to each job. It was a good arrangement.

After talking with the mayor and looking through the jail that first evening on the job, Clay went back to the café hoping to catch Beth before she closed up. He was in luck. She had just blown out the lantern in the kitchen and was headed for the door. He tried the door, but it was locked and the "closed" sign was turned to the street. He knocked. She unlocked the door and invited him in.

"Sorry I don't have anything to offer you. I threw out the rest of the coffee. It was pretty strong anyway. Sit and talk for a while?"

"I'd like that."

"So, you're our new Sheriff I understand."

"Well! News travels fast. I only said yes about an hour ago. How did you know?"

She chuckled, "That's a pretty good clue," and pointed at the badge he had pinned to his vest. He looked down and blushed a bit.

She went on, "But by now, probably half the town knows. Somebody saw that star on your chest as you and the Mayor left the barber shop and he or she told somebody else and so on."

He told her about his conversations with Phil and the mayor and why he hadn't been around all day.

"Jail needs some attention so I guess I'll be cleaning it up for the next couple days before I can spend much time being a Sheriff. Guess I'll go over and try to get a start on it after a while. By the way, part of the deal is that I get three meals per day. Any idea where I might go for those?"

They both laughed and then sat in silence for a moment. Dusk had faded to black outside.

"Clay, I'm glad you're staying. I'll worry about you of course, but I'm glad you're staying just the same."

He took a deep breath and reached across the table to take her hand.

"I'm glad I'm staying, too."

Then, with a slight flash of embarrassment, he gently released her hand and pulled back. She smiled.

"You know, my friend Bert Morgan told me how he met his wife, Annie. She owned a hotel in Santa Fe, and he stayed there. Her hotel had a great little café in it. They sat and talked at one particular table in the place and got to know each other and that's how they fell in love. Kind of like you and me."

He could feel his neck turning red and he quickly added, "Well, I mean like you and me sitting here talking and you owning this place and me staying in the hotel across the street."

She tried unsuccessfully to hide a smile.

He continued, "Anyway, he ended up taking the job of marshal in Santa Fe. Annie still owns the hotel and café even though I think she spends considerably less time in the running of it. Ironic, don't you think?"

Beth said, "Kind of like it was just meant to be for us to be sitting here, isn't it?"

This time she reached across and took *his* hand. Then she laughed and squeezed it.

That's when the door burst open and Doc came rushing in.

"Clay, they just sent word to me to come a runnin', seems there's trouble down by the powder house. Saw you through the window and thought I better tell ya. A no good by the name of Gus Roberts just pistol-whipped old Rodney Cabel. Says old Rodney owes him and he's got a right to take over Rodney's claim and he'll kill any man says different."

"Alright, I'll be along Doc."

Doc ran out and Clay looked at Beth.

"Guess the jail cleaning will have to wait a bit."

"I'll put on a fresh pot of coffee. It'll be ready when you get back," she said.

He smiled at her and stood up, "Might be awhile."

"It'll be ready when you get back," she repeated with a smile.

He stopped in the open doorway, turned back to her for one more look, tipped his hat and went into the darkness.

Neil James

Author Note:

While this is strictly a work of fiction, I have tried to stay true to the times, places and feel of those mountains in the 1800's. The Owyhee Mountains are truly unique. I hope you've enjoyed reading about an area that has changed little. The fact is that its history is rich with everything that has attracted so many of us to the tales of the old west.

About the Author

Neil James is a lifelong resident of Southwestern Idaho. His heritage goes back to the very first days of Silver City. As a youngster, his family spent every possible weekend in the Owyhee high country. As he got older, he ventured off on his own, riding horses and motorcycles in the mountains that stand guard over the river land below. His love of the mountains has never wavered. He spends part of every spring, summer and fall roaming the canyons and high deserts that he writes about.

He lives below the Owyhee Mountains near the Snake River where he is at work on his next novel.

You can contact Neil via email at:
Neil.james.writer@gmail.com
He'll look forward to hearing from you.

Neil James

If you enjoyed reading Vengeance on the Mountain, check Amazon for the next chapter of the Brackett/Morgan series, expected in early 2021. If you would like to be notified when it is available and/or be added to Neil's mailing list, just send a note to:

Neil.james.writer@gmail.com

Made in the USA
Middletown, DE
08 January 2022

58152699R00210